Grievance

Omega Queen Series, Volume 10

W.J. May

Published by Wanita May, 2021.

This is a work of fiction. Similarities to real people, places, or events are entirely coincidental.

GRIEVANCE

First edition. July 15, 2021.

Copyright © 2021 W.J. May.

Written by W.J. May.

Also by W.J. May

Bit-Lit Series
Lost Vampire
Cost of Blood
Price of Death

Blood Red Series
Courage Runs Red
The Night Watch
Marked by Courage
Forever Night
The Other Side of Fear
Blood Red Box Set Books #1-5

Daughters of Darkness: Victoria's Journey
Victoria
Huntress
Coveted (A Vampire & Paranormal Romance)
Twisted
Daughter of Darkness - Victoria - Box Set

Great Temptation Series
The Devil's Footsteps
Heaven's Command
Mortals Surrender

Hidden Secrets Saga
Seventh Mark - Part 1
Seventh Mark - Part 2
Marked By Destiny
Compelled
Fate's Intervention
Chosen Three
The Hidden Secrets Saga: The Complete Series

Kerrigan Chronicles
Stopping Time
A Passage of Time
Ticking Clock
Secrets in Time
Time in the City
Ultimate Future

Kerrigan Memoirs
Chronicles of Devon

Mending Magic Series
Lost Souls
Illusion of Power
Challenging the Dark
Castle of Power
Limits of Magic
Protectors of Light

Omega Queen Series
Discipline
Bravery
Courage
Conquer
Strength
Validation
Approval
Blessing
Balance
Grievance
Omega Queen - Box Set Books #1-3

Paranormal Huntress Series
Never Look Back
Coven Master
Alpha's Permission
Blood Bonding
Oracle of Nightmares
Shadows in the Night

Paranormal Huntress BOX SET

Prophecy Series
Only the Beginning
White Winter
Secrets of Destiny

Revamped Series
Hidden
Banished
Converted

Royal Factions
The Price For Peace
The Cost for Surviving
The Punishment For Deception
Faking Perfection
The Most Cherished
The Strength to Endure

The Chronicles of Kerrigan
Rae of Hope
Dark Nebula
House of Cards
Royal Tea
Under Fire

End in Sight
Hidden Darkness
Twisted Together
Mark of Fate
Strength & Power
Last One Standing
Rae of Light
The Chronicles of Kerrigan Box Set Books # 1 - 6

The Chronicles of Kerrigan: Gabriel
Living in the Past
Present For Today
Staring at the Future

The Chronicles of Kerrigan Prequel
Christmas Before the Magic
Question the Darkness
Into the Darkness
Fight the Darkness
Alone in the Darkness
Lost in Darkness
The Chronicles of Kerrigan Prequel Series Books #1-3

The Chronicles of Kerrigan Sequel
A Matter of Time
Time Piece
Second Chance
Glitch in Time

Our Time
Precious Time

The Hidden Secrets Saga
Seventh Mark (part 1 & 2)

The Kerrigan Kids
School of Potential
Myths & Magic
Kith & Kin
Playing With Power
Line of Ancestry
Descent of Hope
Illusion of Shadows
Frozen by the Future
Guilt Of My Past
Demise of Magic
Rise of The Prophecy
The Kerrigan Kids Box Set Books #1-3

The Queen's Alpha Series
Eternal
Everlasting
Unceasing
Evermore
Forever
Boundless
Prophecy

Protected
Foretelling
Revelation
Betrayal
Resolved
The Queen's Alpha Box Set

The Senseless Series
Radium Halos - Part 1
Radium Halos - Part 2
Nonsense
Perception
The Senseless - Box Set Books #1-4

Standalone
Shadow of Doubt (Part 1 & 2)
Five Shades of Fantasy
Zwarte Nevel
Shadow of Doubt - Part 1
Shadow of Doubt - Part 2
Four and a Half Shades of Fantasy
Dream Fighter
What Creeps in the Night
Forest of the Forbidden
Arcane Forest: A Fantasy Anthology
The First Fantasy Box Set

Watch for more at www.wjmaybooks.com.

Copyright 2021 by W.J. May

THIS E-BOOK OR PRINT is licensed for your personal enjoyment only. This e-book/paperback may not be re-sold or given away to other people. If you would like to share this book with another person, please purchase an additional copy for each recipient. If you're reading this book and did not purchase it, or it was not purchased for your use only, then please return to Smashwords.com and purchase your own copy. Thank you for respecting the hard work of the author.

All rights reserved. No part of this publication may be reproduced, stored in or introduced into a retrieval system, or transmitted, in any form, or by any means (electronic, mechanical, photocopying, recording, or otherwise) without the prior written permission of both the copyright owner and the above publisher of this book.

This is a work of fiction. Names, characters, places, brands, media, and incidents are either the product of the author's imagination or are used fictitiously. Any resemblance to actual person, living or dead, events, or locales is entirely coincidental. The author acknowledges the trademarked status and trademark owners of various products referenced in this work of fiction, which have been used without permission. The publication/use of these trademarks is not authorized, associated with, or sponsored by the trademark owners.

All rights reserved.
Copyright 2021 by W.J. May
Grievance, Book 10 of the Omega Queen Series
Cover design by: Book Cover by Design

No part of this book may be used or reproduced in any manner whatsoever without written permission, except in the case of brief quotations embodied in articles and reviews.

GRIEVANCE

Have You Read the C.o.K Series?

The Chronicles of Kerrigan
Book I - *Rae of Hope* is FREE!

BOOK TRAILER:
http://www.youtube.com/watch?v=gILAwXxx8MU

How hard do you have to shake the family tree to find the truth about the past?

Fifteen year-old Rae Kerrigan never really knew her family's history. Her mother and father died when she was young and it is only when she accepts a scholarship to the prestigious Guilder Boarding School in England that a mysterious family secret is revealed.

Will the sins of the father be the sins of the daughter?

As Rae struggles with new friends, a new school and a star-struck forbidden love, she must also face the ultimate challenge: receive a tattoo on her sixteenth birthday with specific powers that may bind her to an unspeakable darkness. It's up to Rae to undo the dark evil in her family's past and have a ray of hope for her future.

Find W.J. May

Website:
https://www.wjmaybooks.com
Facebook:
https://www.facebook.com/pages/Author-WJ-May-FAN-PAGE/141170442608149
Newsletter:
SIGN UP FOR W.J. May's Newsletter to find out about new releases, updates, cover reveals and even freebies!
http://eepurl.com/97aYf

Grievance Blurb:

USA Today Bestselling author, W.J. May, continues the highly anticipated bestselling YA/NA series about love, betrayal, magic and fantasy.

Be prepared to fight... it's the only option.

The problem with giving everything, is that you end up with nothing left.

When Evie makes a fateful decision, the rest of the realm unites. But her own world is falling apart. Bound in a promise of marriage to a childhood friend, the princess must navigate the politics of the remaining kingdoms while dreaming of Asher and a simpler life on the road.

Things are moving quickly, but there are darker powers at play. A delicate alliance is forming, the forces of good are rallying. But the fate of the kingdoms hangs upon nothing more than a ring.

The enemy is almost upon them. Trouble is brewing on distant shores. Can the princess uphold her promise, or will the cost of such unity prove too great?

Be careful who you trust. Even the devil was once an angel.

The Queen's Alpha Series

Eternal
Everlasting
Unceasing
Evermore
Forever
Boundless
Prophecy
Protected
Foretelling
Revelation
Betrayal
Resolved

The Omega Queen Series

Discipline
Bravery
Courage
Conquer
Strength
Validation
Approval
Blessing
Balance
Grievance
Enchanted
Gratified

– NEW – Beginning's End Series

Check the excerpt at the back of Grievance to see what is coming!!

Chapter 1

What have I done?
Many times in the days ahead, the princess would ask herself that question. It would come back in many volumes, in many voices, in many shades of light. But it would never strike her so clearly as it did in that moment. The moment when thought became reality, and it was a reality that was harsh to the touch. Every inch of her seemed to recoil, rejecting the very essence of the idea though her body remained perfectly still. The die had already been cast. She'd already made the proclamation, asked the question, sealed the fate of three people with the proposed merging of two.

What have I done?

She didn't think she'd ever have an answer.

Not one that would silence the screaming in her heart.

"Asher—"

The name slipped out in barely a whisper, a kind of subconscious plea she hadn't planned on saying aloud. No one could hear it. Since she'd made that fateful proposition, the citadel had only a few seconds of deathly quiet before erupting in a concussion of noise. No one could hear it except the vampire to whom she'd been calling. But he'd stayed for just a fleeting moment, staring between the girl he loved and his shell-shocked best friend before slipping away into the crowd.

The fae was not so lucky.

Caught as he was, *prince* as he was, there was an audience to his every fleeting expression. To each cry of emotion that chased away the last. They came in filters, in a damaging series of degrees.

A rush of confusion, a slap of surprise, a tiny spark of dread—

And then...nothing.

His lovely eyes went blank, staring into hers.

"Is it true, Your Highness?"

Like a changeable tide, the people crowded into the ivory citadel turned from one group of monarchs to another. The younger set. The ones with something left to give.

A hundred pairs of eyes locked upon the fae's stricken face, but try as he might he couldn't answer the question. He couldn't even deflect it. He couldn't find the breath.

"Your Grace." It was the warrior who'd spoken before, the one who stood with a legion of others behind him. "We knew nothing of this proposed alliance." His dark eyes swept curiously between the frozen pair. "Do you wish to make the princess your bride?"

The word swept like wildfire across the gleaming chamber, a blazing inferno hellbent on incinerating anything in its path. It didn't matter that the fae hadn't said a word to confirm it. Nor did it matter that such a thing had been announced without ceremony on the citadel floor.

There were certain things that could electrify a room full of people, arguing alliance while standing on the brink of war. Ironically enough, very few of them had to do with the actual fighting.

Bride.

It leapt from one to the other, swelling in volume, twisting in narrative, until the people standing on the far side of the room were all lifting their voices in the same joyful cry.

The realm was united once again. The Prince of the Fae had found a Belarian bride.

...even if he didn't know it yet.

"Evie."

A quiet voice cut through the clamor. Her best friend from childhood, looking so pale there was a chance he might black out. He stood frozen amidst the swarm, eyes locked upon her face.

"...what are you doing?"

She opened her lips to answer, then a swarm of people surged in between.

"Sweetheart?"

There was no accounting for how Dylan reached her so quickly, not considering he'd been trapped on a podium on the other side of the room. But the moment the eyes of the citadel began to turn, her father was there—angled like a living shield between them.

"What are you..." He trailed off, lifting his hands to the sides of her face before glancing over his shoulder. Ellanden was no help. The young fae had been just as caught off guard as the rest of them, and was rooted to the spot. "This isn't the time, do you hear me? This isn't the time."

She nodded quickly as the rest of the friends were ushered away. The only one who lingered a moment was Freya. The witch was staring in complete astonishment, arms hanging stiff by her sides. When Katerina tried to move her, she blinked quickly before heading the opposite way.

"Your Grace?"

Ellanden lifted his eyes slowly as a company of fae appeared before him. Each face was lit with the same expectant stare, and he suddenly remembered that he'd been asked a question.

Will you marry me?

"I...I don't..."

His skin paled still further as his breathing quickened. Those dark eyes swept frantically over the chamber, searching for a familiar face. An ally to come to his aid. He no longer counted the princess. Some madness had overtaken her, a nightmare that threatened to drag him down as well.

By the same inexplicable magic that had procured Dylan, his own father appeared a moment later—looking as stunned as the rest of them. Fortunately, the Lord of the Fae was never far from that immortal composure. Cassiel stared for only an instant before lifting a hand to the crowd.

"Such a thing has been long discussed," he said quietly, trusting each word to fall upon ready ears, "since they were mere children." He paused a moment, glancing at Dylan, before flicking his hand in such a discreet gesture the others barely noticed. "It is the nature of dark times that such a thing be discussed again, but while I applaud the princess' candor, perhaps it is best to do so behind closed doors. Give everyone a moment to catch their breath."

Such disarming eloquence, enough to soothe even the most excited spirits, yet it was scarcely sufficient for the joyous crowd. Fortunately, Leonor swept down from the podium a moment later to give the finesse a tougher varnish, summoned by that fluttering hand.

"Thus concludes our time together," he announced brusquely, nodding to a pair of guards beside the doors. They opened without delay, filling the chamber with fresh sunlight. "But in due course, you may be summoned again. There are things to prepare. We must make plans."

Cassiel looked at him sharply, and the princess was filled with the sudden certainty that he was not supposed to have added that last part. The two stared at each other a moment before it was Cassiel who turned away—leading his son from the room without a backwards glance.

Dylan stared after them before taking a step to follow.

"Come, Everly," he said under his breath. "We must leave this place."

The others had already departed, slicing their way through the lingering crowd. The princess gripped her father's sleeve, stretching to the tips of her toes to search wildly through the chaos.

"Yes, I just...I just need to find..."

Asher.

For a fleeting moment she thought she saw him, standing near the back of the crowd. Those dark eyes locked onto hers with a look that seared itself forever into memory.

Then, just like that...he was gone.

GRIEVANCE

"WHAT WERE YOU *thinking*?!"

It was a fortunate thing the villa in which the friends were residing sat so high above the rest of the city, but it was still unlikely the citizens of Taviel could fail to hear Katerina Damaris' cry.

"You burst into the citadel, *uninvited*, then propose this lunacy right there on the floor?! It's a wonder no one thought to put a bolt on your bedroom door!"

Evie bowed her head in silence, the same way she'd been standing since the group of them had rushed up the steps of the pavilion and burst inside. There had been scarce few opportunities to get a word in edgewise but, even had it been possible, the princess would have held her tongue.

Her uncle didn't have such qualms.

"Since when does the Princess of the High Kingdom need an invitation to the citadel?" he inserted quietly. "Especially when half the city was already there."

A wave of fire scorched the wall above his head.

"You are *defending* her actions?!" Katerina shrieked.

Her twin stared back with calm patience. "Merely her right to speak."

Almost a half-hour had passed since their departure, but very little had changed. Several members were also conspicuously missing from their group. Cosette and Seth had made themselves deliberately scarce, waiting for tempers to cool down, whilst no one had seen Freya since she set off on her own. Aidan was also absent—searching, no doubt, for his missing son.

But even with their shared bond, the princess had little hope of her uncle finding him. If she had stabbed Asher with a sword, the damage could not have been worse than what she'd done.

"—just don't understand what you were thinking," Katerina muttered again, resuming her ceaseless pacing across the room. "Of all the impulsive, short-sighted things to do—"

There was a soft noise of derision in the corner.

"What was that, Sera?" the queen asked dangerously. "Something you'd like to say?"

All eyes turned to the woodland princess, but she was just as calm as her husband. Perched on the arm of his chair, regarding the manic scene with an impassivity only immortals could achieve.

"I'm saying, perhaps your daughter was not thinking," she answered softly. "Perhaps she simply assessed the situation and saw what needed to be done."

Evie blinked in shock as Cassiel turned to his sister with a dark glare.

"What an easy thing for you to say," he replied coldly. "A natural answer to be given by the *younger* sibling. The one who grew up without worry of such an arrangement herself."

Serafina never flinched. "You accuse the child of impulsivity and short-sightedness, yet have we not been discussing the need for such intervention ourselves? An enemy is fast-approaching, and the realm is divided. Is there a better solution to all our problems? Some card you have yet to play?"

The fae opened his mouth to answer, but Dylan stepped in quickly to intervene.

"Do not be angry with your sister—"

"My *sister* can defend herself," Cassiel interrupted sharply. "And do not presume to meddle in my affairs. That was not the intervention of which we spoke. You and I will not stand here and pretend otherwise. Why you're willing to do so is utterly beyond me—"

"I never claimed to support this venture," Dylan fired back. "But your people did not gather in the citadel out of boredom, Cassiel, just as mine did not refuse our proposed alliance out of an over-developed sense of pride. I would give anything I have to protect the children from any threat or sacrifice that needs to be made, but in this regard I have already taken vows."

A chilling silence followed these remarks, one that frightened Evie more than anything else that had come before. She had only guessed at the extent of Belaria's reluctance, just as she'd merely assumed all was not well with the Fae when they were excluded from the citadel time after time. She didn't know that reluctance had been open refusal. That the Fae had drawn a similar line.

Cassiel's eyes went for only a moment to his son before hardening on his friend anew.

"When such a task was put to us, we refused unequivocally," he said in a low and dangerous voice. One that belied the benevolent uncle and fair-minded lord, and spoke to the restless warrior that lurked underneath. "We refused without question. It's a good thing that I don't share your newfound sense of pragmatism, or that may very well have been your wife sleeping in my bed."

Dylan's eyes flashed, but he did not rise to the challenge. Serafina, on the other hand, pushed to her feet in a burst of exasperation that only her older brother was ever able to bring forth.

"He speaks only in the best interest of the children."

"We have different definitions of the word."

"De luminess se fors—"

"Nesia detithe!"

"ENOUGH!"

Ellanden had been uncharacteristically silent, standing by himself in the corner. No one had dared to approach him, though his father stood automatically in front of him several times.

When he shouted, the room fell silent. When he stepped forward, the others melted back.

But whatever he wanted to say, the words caught like tar in his throat. He simply lifted his gaze, fixing the princess in an unfathomable stare before sweeping suddenly from the room.

She stared for a split second, then took off after him.

THE ROOM WAS BRIGHT with the morning sun when Evie pushed open the door, broken by a single long shadow from where Ellanden stood in front of the window. He tilted his head when she entered, but didn't turn. It wasn't until the door was shut that he circled around suddenly.

"You must take it back."

She paused mid-step, all the apologies and explanations she'd been rehearsing in the hallway dying on her tongue. Her eyes tightened painfully, but he spoke before she could answer.

"Tell them you made a mistake, that you've reconsidered." He shook his head, arms shaking by his sides. "I don't care what you tell them—just find a way to take it back."

She considered him a long moment, then stepped further inside the room. "You prophesized this yourself once," she said softly. "When that grizzled man came to our parents' feast. The matchmaker. You said yourself this might happen. What did you think—"

"I thought we'd have time!" he cried. "I thought we'd escape it! We are heirs to an immortal throne. Short of some tragedy, there would never be cause for such a thing to happen!"

Short of some tragedy? How about a vengeful dragon tearing across the skies?

He took a step towards her just as he'd done a thousand times, then stopped short—that cursed proposal echoing in his head. "Evie...*you* cannot suggest this."

There was something strange about the way he stressed it. A shiver ran up her spine.

"What do you mean?" she asked slowly. "Why could I not—"

"Because there are people who would require it of us," he exclaimed. "There are people who are eager for it. If you give them even the slightest opening..."

He trailed off, eyes shining in the dewy light.

"Everly...*please*. Take it back."

For as often as the fae demanded that things be presented to him, she'd never heard him sincerely ask for something he wanted in his whole life. Not the way he was asking now.

Her breath caught as every fear and doubt manifested into that single word.

"Ellanden—"

"What of Freya?" he interrupted, deliberately cutting her short. "What of Asher? You speak as though this sacrifice would be ours alone, but there are people who would feel it as well. There are people who would live and die by this decision. I do not think they could withstand it."

Like a fading dream, the vampire's voice drifted through the princess' mind.

"Opening your heart to another person, surrendering it so completely... I would imagine it's a bit like that constellation. It's too great a thing to be confined to this place."

A physical pain, like the sting of a dagger, ripped somewhere deep inside. Her chest ached with heaviness. She kept her eyes level, but would not have been surprised if she was bleeding.

"You know I'm right," she said quietly, meeting the fae's piercing gaze. "You've known it from the second we arrived at this place, from the second we arrived in Belaria. Our intentions were pure, but havoc and terror have blossomed in our absence. Lives have been lost. And it is not just those who reside in our capital cities, who walk the halls of the palace... It is those who dwell in the villages, the people who live simple, quiet lives who have felt our departure the most. When the darkness comes—and we know that it will—it will start with them. And it will end them."

Their eyes met in the stillness.

"There is a debt that must be paid. And we are the only ones who can pay it. You think it doesn't pain me to say it? I am asking all the same. If you have any love for me, don't make me beg."

He took a sudden step back, as if that aspect had not yet occurred to him. A war of emotion shadowed across his face, finding no resolution, then he sank abruptly into the nearest chair.

"I would never make you beg," he murmured, face in his hands. "Perhaps you are even right in this. To suggest it takes a bravery that is greater than mine. But Evie...this *cannot* happen."

Their eyes met again and a sudden panic threatened to consume them both.

For what the princess was suggesting was more than a simple alliance. It was more than a rearrangement of titles, a convergence of kingdoms, and a move from one palace to the next.

It was the loss of an eternity...gone in the blink of an eye.

In a flash, the fae was back on his feet—unable to settle in a single place for long. A feverish panic brightened his eyes, and though he walked in sunlight there seemed a shadow about him.

"No," he muttered beneath his breath, "this is lunacy. I can't...I can't even imagine. Things cannot change so quickly. When we left this house, just an hour before, everything was fine—"

"Everything was broken, Landi. I told Seth we weren't at these meetings because they did not yet involve the prophecy. They were only in regards to the crown." She took a step forward, reaching for his hand. "But Ellanden...they are one and the same."

He stared a split second, then wrenched himself away.

What had started in panic had crossed into debate, then ended in a cold rage. It was a look she had seen him wear many times, usually when she was standing by his side.

Never once had it been directed at her.

"*No.*"

He abruptly moved away, turning back only when he was on the far side of the room.

"You're just deciding this?" he challenged. "As if your one voice can speak for us both? I do not *want* this, Everly. That is reason enough for me to fight it, but I will fight it for you as well. You do not desire this union any more than I do. It is a misguided sense of duty from which you spoke, but the kingdoms will come to see reason and so will you."

He stalked to the door and yanked it open.

"As for your proposed marriage...I will never consent to such a thing."

She stood in stunned silence, staring at him across the room. It wasn't until he tilted his head sharply that she realized the door was for her. He was ordering her to leave.

In a kind of daze, she gathered herself and walked silently from the room, trying to remember a time he'd ever dismissed her in such a way before. They would fight, they would bicker, they would laugh, they would conspire...they would never leave.

The door shut the moment she was on the other side, leaving her alone in a deserted hall. A host of tears blurred her eyes and a silent sob wracked her body, bowing her head to her chest.

By the time she lifted it again, she was no longer alone.

Crack.

The slap came out of nowhere, catching her right across the face. Her hair flew back with the force of it and she lifted a trembling hand to her cheek, stunned with the shock and the pain.

Freya didn't say a word, just simply vanished down the hall.

The princess stared after her for a long time, much longer than she realized in the moment, then turned abruptly on her heel and fled to her own chambers. The door swung shut behind her and she threw herself down onto the bed, pressing a pillow over her face as her entire body shook uncontrollably, caught in a never-ending stream of broken-hearted sobs.

When at last she surfaced, the sun had crossed the length of the sky. No one had come to get her. No further commands or instructions had been made. She might have cried even longer, but the moment she stopped she was suddenly certain that it would not start again.

What have I done?

"I have united the realm."

She said the words out loud. She closed her eyes and ached to believe them.

Then lay down in her bed and pretended to sleep.

Chapter 2

Actual sleep remained elusive as the princess lay in bed that night, tracking the moon's progress across the night sky. Not for the first time, she found herself missing those nights with her friends around the campfire. A freedom that felt like a lifetime ago, though it had only been a few short weeks since they'd stumbled into the witch's swamp.

Did Evianna foresee this for me, she thought as she lifted her finger and traced through the constellations, just as she'd done when she was a child. *Did she know we'd end up here, when she made us a portal that day? Did she know of the discord amongst the kingdoms, of the sacrifice that would be required?*

If she had, it seemed a rather important thing to have failed to mention. An unforgivable oversight, though witches were always fond of such things. Reveling in the twists and turns of an ever-mercurial fate. Acting as though they played some great part besides dabbling in entrails and deifying every finished cup of tea.

She thought, in absentminded hypotheticals, it might be nice to ban them unilaterally from the kingdoms. At any rate, it would be prudent. Who knew how many other lunatics were out there right now—erecting invisible carnival tents, speaking in tongues and ruining some girl's life?

When did I start being prudent?

She pushed to her feet with a quiet sigh, crossing the length of her bedroom and pulling open the bureau that stood at the far side. The Fae had a way of gently forcing their culture upon those around them. While the drawers had been stocked with many dresses that had come from the royal seamstresses in Belaria and the High Kingdom, there were silken robes of the fair folk as well.

She lifted a hand to one of them, tracing the gossamer sleeve.

How many times had she seen the eternal members of her family wearing such things growing up? Even her uncle, who did not possess the blood of the royal house, had a similar wardrobe he wore when visiting his wife's native land. She had donned such clothes many times herself, thinking nothing of it, but her mortal friends at the palace had always marveled at the casual enchantment of the Fae. The flowing gowns and airy silks that seemed to float along as one walked.

Would I be required to wear these, she wondered, running the tips of her fingers along the ivory silk. *If Ellanden accepts my proposal...I would be a future queen.*

Strangely enough, the prospect had never occurred to her. Having been born an heir to two of the realm's kingdoms, she'd never felt the urge to lay claim to any others.

Without permission, her eyes drifted out the window to the gleaming streets of the Ivory City. Even from such a distance, she could see the people who resided in the immortal capital making their way to and fro across the polished streets.

How would they react to such news? How would they feel at the sight of a foreign princess wearing those ethereal gowns? Would they decry her as an imposter? Or would they open their arms in welcome to a mortal queen?

Tanya had paved the way, but much as the people of Taviel had grown to love her their general acceptance had far more to do with Cassiel's obvious happiness than the charm of the Kreo priestess herself. The Fae loved a great many people that hadn't been born into their eternal heritage, but that didn't mean they would offer any of them a crown.

But they know me. They've known me since I was a child. Her eyes flickered once again out the window, feeling suddenly like a stranger despite the familiar room. *I basically grew up here.*

An icy chill worked its way into her, rising slowly from the ground. *Does it matter? Ellanden refused. I will never be a queen in Taviel.*

She pushed the traditional garments to the back of her bureau, selecting a simple dress from her mother's kingdom instead. It slipped over her skin with a whisper, swirling to the floor in a cascade of emerald green. She had always favored the color, just like her mother. With their fair skin and crimson locks, it created a brilliant contrast that had grown more distinctive over time. Asher had once told her it looked as though someone had set her aflame, in a most becoming way. He always said it with a teasing grin, the kind that made her giggle and blush. There was one time—

She caught herself suddenly, staring into the mirror. The nostalgic smile faded slowly from her face, leaving a cold sort of emptiness in its wake.

...he will never forgive me.

That was the last time the princess looked in the mirror.

She finished dressing quickly and opened the door, only to freeze with a start. A tall fae was standing just on the other side, his hand still raised to knock.

"Leonor?" she blurted in surprise, taking a step back. Her pulse quickened and she stood up a bit straighter, the way she always did in the elder's presence. "I'm sorry…I wasn't expecting you."

Those immortal eyes swept over her, lingering perhaps a second too long before his face softened in an unexpected smile. "Why should you have been? I sent no message to announce myself." He paused a moment. "It was a rather arduous day at the citadel…I trust you slept well?"

There was a decent chance he knew that she hadn't. Like the rest of his kind, the fae seemed unnaturally adept at intuiting things others couldn't. In her friends, she found this trait to be highly inconvenient. In the renowned statesman…it perfected her posture and quickened her pulse.

Instead of answering, she gestured down the corridor with a strained smile.

"I'm not sure if anyone else is awake yet. I've only just risen myself—"

"I did not come to see the others, Your Highness. I came to see you."

There was a slight variance in his tone, a new way of saying a title she'd heard a thousand times. It took her a moment to realize it had been said with the same deference as when foreign dignitaries and councilmen would address not she and the other children, but their parents.

Because I've altered the game. I've placed myself in a position where I might one day become his queen.

For the life of her, she had no idea if he approved of the idea. As a general rule, fae were hard to read on the best of times, and their head of counsel was perhaps the very worst.

"I wondered if the three of us might speak," he continued, eyeing her with the same regard in which she'd been examining him. "Just a quick conversation, then you may return to your day."

There was no need to ask to whom he was referring. Since she'd been unceremoniously banished into the corridor, the prince's name had never really left her mind.

Her gaze dropped suddenly to the ground.

"He won't speak to me," she said softly.

Leonor paused, staring down at her with an appraising eye.

The ageless fae had been at the helm of his people for more centuries than the little princess could possibly imagine. He'd seen them through countless atrocities, guided them through the subsequent reconstructions, been a lone voice for peace in a room full of tempers and the first to put on his armor when that peace gave way to war. He was a living memory, the elder of all Fae.

But he was looking at the princess with something close to respect.

"That was not an easy thing you did," he said quietly, dark eyes flickering in the soft light. "I remember the day you were born, Everly. I've watched you and Ellanden since you were children, playing together in the sun. I know you do not feel for each other the way a husband and wife should. But you didn't make this decision as a wife. You made it as a future queen."

He paused another moment, letting the words settle.

"Ellanden will understand this...eventually. He will come round."

Evie nodded faintly, but she didn't know if that was remotely true. She pictured the fae in his bedroom—glaring at the door and clutching his ficus.

"Do you think I was wrong?" she called suddenly, as Leonor began walking away. A blush stole into her cheeks, but she held his gaze. "Do you think I was wrong to have done it?"

She would never have asked the fae under normal circumstances, but she also would never have imagined he'd come to her door. The two stared at each other a long moment, then he lifted his arm, gesturing for her to walk along by his side.

"I think it may be the only way."

THE TWO MADE A QUICK pass through the house, then left the villa entirely—pausing on the top of the pavilion stairs. It was a quieter morning than the one that had come before. No more strained conversations, no more shouting matches in the citadel. Things were tranquil, calm.

And yet there was a charge to the air she was only beginning to understand.

"I don't know where Landi is," she blurted suddenly, realizing she probably should have said this right from the start. Her eyes flickered without permission to Asher's bedroom. "I don't know where anyone is." She pulled in a quick breath. "He might still be sleeping."

He might be sharpening a blade.

Leonor smiled ever so slightly, as if he was privy to her thoughts. His dark eyes closed and he tilted his head for a moment, walking with sudden purpose towards the balcony.

She followed in silence behind him, wondering how he knew which way to go.

It came as no surprise that the fae was indeed on the terrace, arms resting lightly upon the railing as he gazed in silence over the side. He startled when they joined him, turning around swiftly.

"Deaso sai," he greeted Leonor, straightening in surprise. "No one told me you were..." He trailed off when he saw the princess, stilling with sudden anger. "Did you send for him?!"

She flinched at the venom in his voice, opening her mouth quickly to deny it. But the stately fae spoke before she could—resting an unexpected hand upon her shoulder.

"I came of my own choosing," he replied calmly, tilting his head with a slight frown. "And I am very much surprised you would take such a tone with your friend."

Of all the people in the five kingdoms, the councilman was perhaps the only one with the latitude to scold a High-Born prince. A faint blush appeared in Ellanden's cheeks, and though his eyes flashed in a muted version of that same rage he kept his silence and lowered his gaze.

"I sought out the princess this morning so that the three of us might have a frank discussion," the elder continued abruptly, gesturing to a table and chairs. "Please...sit."

Not exactly an invitation. More of a gracious command.

The two youngsters eyed each other for a moment then pulled out seats at opposite sides of the polished table, keeping the councilman firmly in between. He glanced a moment at each one then settled himself down slowly, moving with a deliberately unhurried grace.

Long seconds passed before he turned to Ellanden.

"You have been given a shock."

The prince's eyes flashed up, though what he meant to say was uncertain.

In days gone past, he might have been looking at his greatest ally. Despite his stiff exterior, Leonor's indulgence knew no bounds when it came to the boy. He'd spoiled him ceaselessly, praised his accomplishments, forgiven his sins. When Ellanden had stolen his father's horse at the age of four, the young prince had actually fled in terror to hide within the councilman's chamber.

But he was no longer a child. And different things were required.

"Though the shock is really mine," Leonor continued with a twinkle. "I am your head counsel. You might have provided me some warning before making such a proclamation."

Bold move to start with a joke, but he may have misread his audience.

Ellanden took a deep breath, gripping the edge of the table as if it was the only thing left tethering him to the world. He was quiet a moment, perhaps he was counting.

Then he lifted his head.

"Leonor...you must believe me. I cannot do such a thing." The elder fae stared at him in silence, until his pulse began to race. "I'm not lying—"

The councilman held up a hand.

"Peace, child."

A hush of silence fell over the table, one that cut through the jokes and invitations to the raw emotions underneath. Leonor studied young fae carefully, his eyes taking in every inch.

"Too long you've been away from this city," he murmured. "Taking shelter in different kingdoms, travelling the wilderness with your friends. But you're still a fae." He stressed the word carefully. "The prince of these people, and all that it entails. You could not lie to me if you wished. I know exactly what this sacrifice means...but you must do it anyway."

"No, I cannot—"

"You cannot stand beside an altar and repeat an elder's words? You cannot take the hand of this girl you've loved since you were children, kiss her face, and in doing so...save the entire realm?"

Two sets of eyes came together.

"Yes, Ellanden," he said softly. "I think you can do that."

Another silence came over them, but this time the fae was unable to keep his seat. He sprang from the table, pacing wildly before whirling back around to the elder's chair.

"Why is such a thing even necessary?" he hissed. "A *dragon* is bearing down upon us and he brings hell upon his wings. If the people of this land do not fight together, they will perish! A child could understand the logic! And yet they must wait for a ring to be forced onto my finger?"

Evie bent her head carefully at the table, staring at her fingers. In the chaos at the citadel, she had forgotten several key components of what she was suggesting.

There would be a wedding. There would be a ring.

Leonor again held up a hand for silence, nodding thoughtfully as if to temper the prince's rage. He waited until Ellanden had sat back down before continuing his quiet contemplations.

"When you first arrived, you asked if we could speak as we once did. From the pieces I've already heard, you have quite the story. But I have a story to tell you as well."

He paused for breath.

"Cadarest was sacked. Shortly after came Nimiel and the Western Crest. The giants have overrun Saddreah, and those living in the northern settlements have begun to flee to the coast."

Ellanden stared back in shock, no color left in his face. "You jest," he said faintly, unable to believe its truth. "You're trying to make a point—"

"They were unspeakable losses," Leonor interrupted quietly. "Ones that may well have been prevented. Ones we had aimed to remedy in time. But with a new darkness on the horizon…"

He trailed off, leaving the young fae to imagine the worst.

A rather crude strategy in terms of transparency, but under no circumstance did the elder intend to mislead or manipulate the prince into doing his bidding. He was merely presenting the facts. They made his case for him and were damning enough.

"All the more reason…" Ellanden stammered, trying to find his footing, "all the more reason to forget these newfound divisions and fight together as a whole. If our people have suffered such losses, those sustained by the rest of the kingdom must be tenfold. *That* is reason enough for an immediate and lasting alliance, Leonor. Why must there be a ceremony to—"

"Each of those settlements fell in violation of some treaty. Each of them came about not only by the invasion of an enemy, but the painful absence of a friend. Such things cannot be easily forgiven, Ellanden. Such trust is not rebuilt overnight. By uniting the four kingdoms, the pair of you can single-handedly build in a day what months of toiling on a battlefield could never achieve."

He leaned forward in earnest, reaching for the prince's hand.

"It is justice, what I am asking. A chance for your people to reclaim what has been lost and settle old grievances. It is the promise of a future for all that would be doomed if you choose to stay in your chambers on the appointed day, instead of kissing a bride in the Celestial Hall."

Ellanden flinched as the man's voice rose in anger, but at no point did he back down. He merely turned his head, as if his trusted friend was too painful to look at straight on.

"It is an *eternity* that you're asking," he corrected softly, lifting his eyes to the distant sky. A kind of sadness had taken hold of him, settling somewhere deep inside. "I love another. There is—"

"I know of Freya," the elder interrupted gently. "But my dear boy, now you are speaking of two different things. Either such a union is politically unnecessary, or you couldn't stand the loss of your beloved witch. Because, Ellanden, I'm here to tell you...such a union *is* politically necessary."

He reached across the table, lifting the fae's chin.

"And as for the rest, you must ask yourself what's more important...your own happiness, or the life of every man, woman, and child living in the realm."

This time, the silence was final. There seemed no breaking it.

Leonor let it hang over the table before pushing to his feet.

"The carionelle is already within the city. Will you agree at least to speak with him?"

Ellanden couldn't answer, he simply nodded his head.

The councilman swept down the pavilion steps a moment later, leaving the two friends frozen at the table, silently drowning on either side.

After a long stretch of time, the fae lifted his eyes.

"What am I going to say to Freya?"

He was so lost that, for a moment, he forgot to be angry. He simply looked at the princess with those haunted, searching eyes. She shook her head, staring at the cracks in the table.

What am I going to say to Asher?

Chapter 3

For a long time the princess and the fae sat on the terrace, staring in opposite directions. Each one growing steadily more resentful of the inherent beauty of the place.

The soft radiance of dawn had been replaced with the bolder, clearer colors of a rising new day—wisps of ivory clouds, dappled patterns of watery sunlight, and skies of such a reflective blue the princess half-imagined she could see herself watching from the other side. A gentle breeze stirred the air around them, bringing with it the sweet fragrance of a thousand flowers, and not a full minute could pass without hearing the ringing call of the island's native birds.

So different these animals were from those who roamed the lands of Belaria and the High Kingdom. Those beasts seemed to have leapt straight off the page of stories—regal stags and clever foxes, packs of roving wolves, and bears that stood nearly as high as the village houses. The princess had always found a strange comfort in that, the predictability of it. It seemed to her the *real* world.

But everything in Taviel had come from the stars.

From the iridescent clouds of butterflies that drifted across the sky, to the long, silver cats that hunted at midnight and prowled the tops of the trees, right to down to the domesticated herds of snow-white deer with eyes so large and knowing they struck her almost as people.

It was said that not much had survived after the First Age of Darkness had swept over the land. After the great lords of the fae had driven back the creatures of the Dunes and restored a tentative peace, it was the princess' own ancestors who had broken it. Who'd burned the Ivory City to the ground and ferried giants across the tranquil sea to destroy the very foundations so it could never be rebuilt. But the Fae *did* rebuild. And it all started with the arrival of a heron.

"What are those called?" she broke the silence abruptly, gazing up at a trio of birds. They were the same kind that perched outside her bedroom window. Tiny songbirds with green-tipped wings and a shining amethyst chest—like they'd been carved from gemstones and breathed to life.

Ellanden lifted his head slowly, as if he'd been roused from a deep sleep. He glanced only a moment at the singing birds before pushing to his feet and striding away from the terrace.

"They're called Narsi," he answered without looking. "It means hope."

Evie stared after him, clinging to the arms of her chair. Then she pulled in a deep and deliberate breath before pushing to her feet as well, heading in the opposite direction.

It was a new thing—this forced breathing. An odd sensation to administer something so involuntary, but there was a steadiness in doing so as well. No one could see it, no one could feel it, no one could control it except her. For one of the first times in her life, she wondered with vague curiosity at the people who were gathered even now along the shores of the river—staring in silent reflection, lifting their voices in song. Taviel was known for such meditative contemplation—people journeyed for weeks just to sit beside those sparkling waters and gain some elusive insight they had otherwise missed. She had always much preferred the archery range, having no time for such rumination herself. But perhaps there was something more to it. Perhaps she would go there now...

"*Careful.*"

She rounded the corner and tipped off her feet at the precise moment that Seth reached down and caught her, hands lingering on her shoulders until she'd steadied herself once more.

"You good?"

Having no possessions or wardrobe himself, the shifter was wearing things borrowed from Ellanden, missing his worn leathers and fidgeting a bit uncomfortably in a silken tunic. His hair fell loose to his shoulders, free of its usual braids, and one hand kept drifting involuntarily to his belt.

The princess watched him for a second, then forced a smile. "Feels strange not to wear a sword?"

He dropped his hand immediately, coloring with a faint blush. "I was...politely relieved of my weapons upon arrival," he admitted. "I managed to sneak in a few small daggers, but everything else was considered uncouth for the city streets."

Evie laughed softly as he quoted words that were most decisively not his own.

Considering the Fae spent just as much time training with weapons as they did gazing pensively at the stars, they didn't exactly appreciate that skill in others—at least, not when they were guests within the Ivory City's walls. Call it post-traumatic stress disorder, or merely a common sense of precaution, considering how many times the city had been attacked. But unless one carried what the Fae considered an elegant weapon—bows and arrows—they were surrendered upon arrival.

"Don't take it personally," she said lightly, glancing over her shoulder as those tiny birds took off into the clouds. "Even the royal household is disarmed when they visit. Leonor takes great pleasure in confiscating my father's weapons himself..."

Her smile faded as the councilman's face drifted through her mind.

So the matchmaker was already within the city? When had he been summoned? Was it the moment the children were discovered to be alive, or did they wait a full week before—

"Are you all right?"

She glanced up suddenly, to see Seth looking down at her with quiet concern. His brow was furrowed and those dark eyes made a worried study of her face.

"None of us was expecting..." He trailed away himself, searching for the words. "I didn't know you were planning something like that when we headed for the citadel."

"I wasn't," she said softly, looking down at her shoes. "It sort of burst out of me when I saw what was happening, when I heard what the people had to say." She paused a moment, almost too frightened to continue. "...have you seen Asher?"

The shifter's face went still before he shook his head. "Not since yesterday. He was gone by the time the rest of us got outside. Cosette was thinking of looking for him, but I think your uncle—"

Evie nodded quickly, tucking back her hair. "Aidan will find him."

It's an island. Even a vampire can't hide forever.

...unless he decides to swim.

Seth stared down at her a moment longer, then asked his question again.

"Are you all right?"

She opened her mouth to answer, armed with another of those measured breaths. Then her face crumpled and she shook her head—biting her lower lip, while her eyes spilled over with tears.

"Oh, honey..."

One of the best things about making friends with someone who wasn't born in a royal city was that he didn't subscribe to royal city rules. Seth gathered her swiftly in his arms, just as if they'd been back in the woods, holding her steady as she buried her face in his shirt and cried. The sobs wracked her entire being, one after another, her thin frame trembling. It went on so long she felt almost dizzy for lack of breath, but he never faltered. He simply held her—rocking them back and forth, smoothing down the back of her hair, until she felt strong enough to stand again on her own.

"You know," he murmured, "I was jealous when I first met all of you. The *royal* family, right there in the flesh. You'd never known hunger, never known sickness. You'd never stayed up late at night with a candle, trying to teach yourself how to read. The things that troubled you...they were so different from the things that troubled me. I didn't really understand them."

She wiped her cheeks, flushed and shaken. "...and now?"

He flashed a sad smile, keeping the answer to himself.

"How about we get some food?" he suggested, lifting his arm to escort her away from the terrace. "My guess is you haven't eaten since yesterday morning, and you're kind of a nightmare when you're hungry."

She laughed in spite of herself, still trying to catch her breath.

The man was wearing strange clothes, in a strange land, surrounded by strange people who spoke a strange language. But he was still keeping track of whether she had managed to eat.

It made her want to embrace him. She threatened him instead.

"Careful. I might have my guards beat you in a fit of over-privileged rage."

"Ah, but would they have any weapons?" he countered, leading them down the steps to the courtyard. "Because I'm pretty confident of my chances—"

The pair leapt back with a gasp.

No sooner had they set foot upon the polished stone than an eruption of sparks sliced the air straight ahead of them—searing it open like the carving of a knife. A blinding arch appeared, one that both friends had a sneaking suspicion they'd seen before. But no sooner could they think to call someone—or better yet, run screaming from the villa—than a mottled hand shot into the air.

"A little help?"

The voice was wretched, repulsive, withered with age. There was also laughter in it. And distance. And a wisdom that was perhaps out of reach to anyone but the elders themselves.

"Sakes alive—I believe I'm stuck!"

Seth took a quick step backwards, muttering something about disembodied limbs and lessons his mother had taught him, while the princess stepped forward with a secret smile. Her fingers wrapped around ones that were so cracked and knobby they could scarcely be counted as fingers at all, then she gave a sharp tug. There was a cloud of dust, followed by a hacking cough.

Then a spectral figure pulled itself from the sparks.

"My darling girl...what a fine mess you've made."

It was a woman—that much was made clear. At least, she had been a woman in some past configuration, but now she was closer to memory and dust. A marbled face peered forth from beneath a mountain of snowy white hair and, given the extreme petiteness of her frame, the princess wasn't quite sure how she was managing to stand beneath the crushing weight of so many shawls.

But none of that mattered, because this creature was a friend.

In spite of the darkness creeping towards them, in spite of the thundering storms in her own clear blue skies, Evie found herself leaning down with a genuine smile.

"Always a pleasure, Gran."

The two embraced warmly, matched for strength. The Kreo priestess might have been a living fossil, but like all such things preserved by magic there was an unnatural grit to her as well.

"Gran?" Seth repeated faintly, still a bit shaken by the sight. "As in...Ellanden's gran?"

The old woman released her immediately, pulling back with a theatrical gasp to gawk at the handsome young shifter. Her eyes swept shamelessly up and down, lingering on choice parts.

"By all the angels in heaven—"

Evie squeezed her arm with a grin. "Easy, Gran..."

For his part, Seth was mildly terrified. The portal had been shocking enough, and this woman seemed to have been summoned straight from the grave. She stared with a brazen intensity until he began to fidget, then she extended her hand with an absurd and grandiose smile.

"Allow me to introduce myself." Her knobby fingers squeezed around his own. "My name is Lavinia Nicholiana Sombritzia Tagoria Oberon. High Priestess of the Kreo."

He caught his breath and shook slowly, afraid to squeeze her hand. "I'm...Seth."

The princess stifled a secret grin, remembering their conversation in Belaria. She'd be willing to bet that right about now the shifter wished he'd at least a last name to offer in return.

But the ancient priestess beamed in delight.

"*Seth*?" she repeated suggestively, running her thumb across the top of his hand. "This wouldn't be the same *Seth* who stole the heart of our dear little Cosette? Condemned to fight in the gladiatorial pits of Tarnaq, only to be freed with a string of diamonds and an immortal kiss?"

His eyes flashed in panic to Evie, who wrenched them apart with a grin.

"One and the same. And you're certainly well-informed," she couldn't help but add, looking the woman up and down. "How exactly did such news reach you? You had to use a portal to get here, it's not like we could have sent a raven—"

"You *insult* me with such logistics," she interrupted, winking at the shifter and adjusting her rather questionable crown. It looked as though at some stage it might have been a rabbit. "And I'm afraid you'll find me *quite* well-informed." Those sharp eyes flew to the princess. "For example, it's recently come to my attention that you've tried to make an honest man out of my only grandson."

A ringing silence fell over the trio before the woman flashed a toothy smile.

"...good luck."

FOR THE NEXT FEW HOURS, Evie stole away into an abandoned sitting room and poured out her heart and soul to the oldest living member of the Kreo. Taking her through every limited memory of the last ten years, heaping on so many extraneous details she felt utterly exhausted by the end.

Considering the woman's eccentricity and flares of emotion, she was surprisingly quiet, listening in virtual silence until the princess concluded her fantastical tale. Once she had, they sat a few minutes in silence. Then the woman nodded abruptly and lifted her head.

"So you decided to propose?"

Evie leaned back in her chair, feeling a little off-balance.

"I didn't *decide* anything," she replied. "I just...after everything we'd seen, everything we'd heard...I didn't see what else could be done."

It wasn't until that very moment, sitting with the old chief beside the remains of a mid-day fire, that the princess realized how long the decision had been in the making. Ever since the three of them woke up in that cave and Cosette kept saying how the world had changed. Ever since they sat down in that tavern and saw the blank, unsurprised faces of the other patrons when a gang burst through the door with the intention to rob them all blind. So many tiny travesties and here they were, standing on the precipice of one of the greatest ones of all.

"Oh, my dear..." Gran sat up slowly, rubbing her eyes. The shifter had been dismissed long before and the two had spent the hours to themselves. "You remind me..."

She trailed off with an unexpected chuckle.

"What?" Evie asked with unrestrained curiosity. There had been several points during the conversation when the woman hung her head with a weary sigh. There had been several more when she'd cried. The last thing the princess had been expecting was a smile. "I remind you of what?"

The old woman sat back in her chair, surveying the girl in front of her.

"You remind me of your mother, when we met so long ago." Her eyes flickered with a spark of times gone by. "She was...*riddled with ad-*

venture, for lack of a better way of putting it. She was tired, she was frightened, and your father was never very far from her hand."

Evie stared at her a moment, then bowed her head.

"...it's not what I imagined."

That was putting it mildly. For as many times as the princess had dreamt of embarking upon an adventure of her own, she never would have thought it might turn out like this.

The Kreo stared back with equal intensity.

"It never is," she crackled, warming her hands by the flames. "But in this case, my darling, I believe the fates might have been acting in our favor."

Evie shook her head in confusion.

"How do you mean?" she countered. "I've proposed marriage to one of my two best friends, the friend I'm *not* in love with. He hates me now. Freya hates me. I'd say that Asher hates me, but to be honest he's gone missing, so I'm not really sure. I'm fairly sure the people are on my side, but if my visions of this dragon are true I'm about to lead them all to certain death. So tell me again how these fates are acting in our favor? Because I'd honestly prefer they left us alone."

The chief laughed to herself, then reached out to take the princess' hand.

"All that may well be true...but you have come home to us. And all these dreadful problems of which you speak may be solved with nothing more than the exchange of a ring."

Her eyes twinkled with an ancient smile.

"That seems rather fortunate to me..."

Chapter 4

Despite the length of time that Evie had spoken with the Kreo chief, there were still long hours to wait before her agreed-upon meeting with the matchmaker. The *carionelle*—she had to keep reminding herself the Fae word for it. Not that the man was fae. For that matter, she wasn't sure he was technically a man. Their only previous encounter had left a rather stilted impression. And given that he'd apparently carried the title since the dawn of time, there was no telling what he might be.

Ellanden had joked he was some kind of lizard.

When we were still speaking. When he still told me jokes.

She let out a quiet sigh, pacing in tight circles around her room.

Her mother had come by earlier to 'check in' and 'apologize' for their previous fight. Neither were exactly her strong suit. If it hadn't been for the previous day's events, the princess might have laughed. She wasn't sure if the queen would be accompanying her to the meeting. In the preliminary discussions, women were typically excluded from such an event. She could count upon the presence of her father but, given the nature of what they were discussing, she wasn't sure he'd be much help.

That just left Cassiel…and Ellanden.

She sighed again as she thought of the seething fae. Never had she seen him so profoundly upset, as if she'd shaken his very foundations. Despite his whimsical and oftentimes arrogant facade, there was a true kindness that lay underneath. An unguarded kind of sweetness that couldn't be taught and was even less often shown. But, rare as it was, that was the side of him she knew best.

If they had come to this decision together or, even worse—if they had been *forced* into it together—they would be coping together as well. His rants and refusals would be echoed in even greater volume by her own. They would have made plans to skip the meeting entirely and would be halfway through a stolen bottle of spirits—hiding somewhere (though never calling it that), and plotting their escape, whilst boldly vowing to never be captured by the bonds of marriage.

He would have been a solace, an ally, a crutch. For much as she loved Asher, there was no one better than the fae to soothe frayed nerves. They could have been all that to each other...if only she hadn't stepped into that citadel. If only she hadn't said those fateful words herself.

But we ARE being forced into it, she corrected herself sharply. *And I wasn't the first to suggest this union, only the first to bring the plan to light. Can he truly think I would ever consider such a thing on my own?*

A hint of anger swept through her, but she was quick to shut it down.

She hadn't told him, after all. Here she was lamenting the fact they weren't partners in a shared misery, but she'd taken that first giant step on her own—leaving him lost in the aftermath.

But even that wasn't premeditated, she argued with herself again, refusing to shoulder all the blame for such a notion—not when she was so thoroughly repelled by it herself. *It was a spur of the moment decision. One that's rooted in nothing but sacrifice and dire need—*

She sat down abruptly on the bed, unwilling to debate with herself any longer.

Am I to have NO allies in this?

First the surprise appearance of Leonor, then the startling arrival of Gran...out of all the characters sweeping about the villa they were the ones with whom she'd least expected to share any personal discussion on the matter, yet they'd both deliberately sought her out. So overwhelmingly, *dramatically* different the two were, yet in some regards they were exactly the same.

Pillars of strength. Pillars of community. And both of them touched by a distant kind of magic; the kind that lingered only fleetingly in the present before setting its sights on the horizon.

She'd clung to the support, but she'd also half-wanted them to stop her. What did it mean when such a pair was in agreement over anything, let alone something like this? They'd lived long enough to know it needed to be done, and they wanted their respective peoples to live long enough to channel such a union into a great and lasting peace. Given the bloodlines in question, there could be nothing stronger. It was perhaps the single greatest chance at peace that the realm had ever seen.

She'd wanted them to stop her, yet maybe she'd simply needed them to hold her hand. It was beyond all of them, a decision like this. The ramifications would stretch past individual people and outlast the weight of crowns. It was a proposal not of marriage, but of a future. One that was bathed in light and goodness. A gift for every man, woman, and child in the five kingdoms.

Even her parents—her stubborn, noble parents—knew it had to be done. Her mother could yell and curse, her father could battle his friends and stand in between, but they both knew it had to be done. They'd known since they set foot in Belaria. They'd probably known it even earlier, from the second that fiery dragon touched down from the sky.

The land was broken. It needed healing.

If only everyone could see it the same way—

She lifted her head sharply, turning towards the window.

The room was perfectly silent, but it was though someone had called her name. Rather, it *felt* as though someone had called her. Even now it lingered, tugging her from somewhere deep inside.

She took a step forward, then another. When she reached the balcony, she glanced swiftly in either direction then leapt straight over the side. The courtyard was just a short drop below, but she didn't linger. The second her feet touched the stone, she was up and moving again—this time, away from the villa and into the mountains above. This time, with a particular target in mind...

SHE KNEW THE VAMPIRE was there before she could see him, the same way she'd felt his silent presence without having to actually hear the call. Like a hunter who'd scented prey she ghosted up the slippery peak of the mountain, lifting her face as the spray of the falls misted down from above.

They were very close now to where Ellanden had taken them the night after the feast, when a young fae in the dining hall had snubbed her and she needed to calm down. It had been a beautiful end to an otherwise unsettling evening. Free from the whispers and stares of the crowd the friends had stood together in contended silence, gazing up at the brilliant constellations trailing the sky.

Asher had taken her aside as they were leaving, given her a string of white gemstones she abruptly realized she was still wearing that very day. They dug into her neck the second she thought of them, hanging with a weight she didn't remember them having before.

The leaves grew dense as she left the path behind. Several of those lovely flowers turned out to have thorns. But she knew she was close. A second later, she saw a dark head of hair.

"Asher?"

The vampire jumped around, eyes wide with surprise. His people were almost impossible to startle, but his mind had been drifting miles away. He stood there a moment, caught in a wordless stare, then stepped down from the ledge upon which he'd been standing.

"How did you..."

"I sensed you," she said a bit breathlessly, still dizzy with the sensation. "I could feel that you were up here. I think...I think it was our bond."

Not until she said the words out loud did she actually make the connection. Quite possibly because that wasn't how bonds were supposed to work. Not for the mortal side, anyway. Aidan had been able to track the others from the moment he tasted their blood, but it never worked in reverse.

It was quiet for a few seconds.

"That's odd," Asher finally managed.

Her eyes flashed to his face, then she bowed her head—nodding quickly. For a fraction of a second, she'd actually forgotten the reason she came. She'd forgotten the reason he'd left.

Another chilling silence fell between them, even harder than the last.

How do I even begin?

"I'm glad I found you," she murmured softly. "I almost went out looking last night, but I didn't think I'd find you. And I figured you might want a bit of space…"

The vampire gave not the slightest reaction. He merely stood in front of her, staring with those enormous, unfathomable eyes.

"Ash…I wasn't planning on doing it. I didn't *want* to do it. It wasn't until we were standing in the citadel that I realized…" She shook her head in silence, tears springing to her eyes. "All those people, in all those different kingdoms. You heard what they said, they were never going to agree to an alliance. Kaleb Grey is out there, we've already seen what he can do. And if they wouldn't fight together…" She trailed off helplessly, risking another look at his face. "Asher…I'm so sorry."

Please, say something.

His eyes were red, though he hadn't been crying. The color stood in stark contrast to the fairness of his skin, making it look as if he'd been hit. Maybe he had. No matter whether they made it through this storm or not, the princess didn't think she'd ever known where he'd been that night.

It should have been a warning, but it made him all the more beautiful.

Vampires were like that. A touch of friction, the slightest bit of flux, and all that chaos and churning and combustion were magnified in the brilliant luminance of their eyes. It sucked one in closer, like the pull of a dying star. Evie felt its power now, a magnetism made even stronger by the power of their bond. She felt like it would blind her, kill her. Make her never want to smile again.

She needed to be with him. She needed to be close—

"Get away from me."

She froze in perfect stillness, staring in surprise. She hadn't realized that she'd taken a step towards him. Not until those quiet words scalded the air.

He stared at her a moment, then his lips quirked in a terrible smile.

"I just keep waiting for the rest of it."

Her head shook in confusion.

"The rest—"

"But she wasn't *really* proposing, the princess had a plan." His eyes flashed as he took a step forward, narrating in a voice that wasn't his own. "She never intended to go through with it, she was merely buying time until the armies could be assembled and the battle could be won. It was a trick, a postponement. A ruse of some kind. You know…the *rest* of it."

He stopped a few feet away, and for just a flicker of an instant the princess could see past the barbs and the anger to the raw, unmitigated heartbreak that lay just beneath.

"But there is no rest of it," he concluded softly, "is there?"

She sank her teeth into her lower lip, shaking her head. "Ellanden and I are meeting with the carionelle this evening."

He jerked like he'd been slapped, then took a quick step back.

From that point on, it was like he had trouble looking at her. He began pacing just as she'd done in her chambers, and even when he faced her straight on it was like a part of him wasn't there.

"Well, there you have it," he said abruptly, trembling from head to toe. He opened his mouth to say something further, then merely shook his head. "And Ellanden agreed?"

I wouldn't say that.

"He needed some convincing," she admitted, eyes locked on the ground. "At first, he flat-out refused and threw me out of his room...but then Leonor talked with him the next morning."

She wanted to say more. She wanted to reiterate all those points the councilman had made back on the terrace. Recounting the tales of loss and sorrow, repeating the necessity for such a treaty in that same quiet, unfaltering voice. But she couldn't bear to go through it again.

And Asher didn't want to hear it.

"Of course he could be convinced," the vampire said bitterly, still pacing in angry lines across the ground. "He holds himself responsible for the loss of that Kreo village. The one my people burned. You tell him that an entire kingdom of villages will perish the same way unless he recites a few words? Of *course* he could be convinced."

Whether or not he viewed the fae's bereaved conscience in any kind of esteem, it was impossible to say. But judging from what happened next, the princess was willing to be against it.

"If he thinks I'll eventually forgive him—he's wrong. If he goes through with this, if he sets a single foot inside that chapel...it's over between us. He'll be dead to me."

It was a strange thing for a vampire to say. But as loosely as he'd begun throwing around phrases like 'my people', Asher wasn't like most vampires.

Most were rootless, nomadic. They came and went as they pleased, like a mercurial wind or a rogue tide. They were primal, things of nature. As such, they saw the world in a different way.

The opinions of others didn't matter. Most didn't stay in one place long enough to form attachments. It was the mark of true chaos to venture such a dangerous and contrary opinion, to form any kind of permanence beyond oneself. To even consider the idea of family?

Evie stared a moment, then lowered her eyes. "You don't mean that. You have loved each other since—"

"Love?!" Asher interrupted fiercely. "This coming from a girl who kissed me under the stars, then woke up the next morning and proposed to my best friend. All due respect, Everly, you have lost the freakin' right to tell me a thing about *love*."

She flinched and kept her eyes on the ground, letting him say his piece.

"You didn't even tell me! You marched us all into that room, echoed some promise about us always staying together, then offered yourself in *marriage* to someone else!"

His voice rang over the forest, echoing in the trees.

"Is that even registering with you? Because you seem *irritatingly* calm!"

She held up her hands, forcing herself to meet his eyes.

"I'm not," she swore. "I promise, I'm not calm. I'm a whole mess of things right now, but none of them is calm. And I can never tell you truly sorry I am for announcing it like that. I just—"

"For *announcing* it like that?" he repeated incredulously, forgetting himself for a moment and taking her hand. "Evie...it's the *marriage*. It's the *wedding*. It's *everything* that comes next."

She sucked in a quick breath, clinging to his fingers. "I know, and I've spent a lot of time thinking about that." She breathed again, shaking to the tips of her shoes. "Asher...I don't see how anything really has to change."

The moment she said it, she knew it was wrong. That light in his eyes, the one that was open and weeping and begging her to see reason, went suddenly dim.

"Hear me out—"

He pulled his hands away.

"Ash, it's only a ceremony," she insisted. "It's only a ring, it's only a dress. So Ellanden and I will sit on matching thrones—what does that matter to *us*?"

He shook his head slowly and his eyes locked upon her face.

"Are you really asking me that?" he said softly. "Is that how you think it will be? You'll spend the day holding my hand, then go to sleep in his bed?"

She bit her lip until she tasted blood, wiping away tears with the back of her hand.

"We can live in separate kingdoms," she insisted, "just the way we did before. We'll only see each other when formality requires it. He can be with Freya. I can be with you—"

"And what of the rest of it?"

Their eyes came together and a hush fell over the wood.

"You will have a child with him? His child. His and yours. Not mine."

His voice broke and it ripped through her like a dying breath.

Never once had they talked about such a thing. In truth, she didn't even know if that was something he'd ever wanted. But looking at him now, the answer was clear to see.

"I'm just...I'm just trying to do what I can. To make the best of—" She cut short when he started walking away, staring at the back of his head. "This will save *countless* lives, Asher."

He paused, staring over the falls. "And it will destroy a few others."

A wave of sadness wilted his shoulders, one that was equal parts resignation and despair. He spoke again without turning, drowning his gaze in that endless chasm of mist.

"How long could it last, anyway? A princess and a vampire."

A wistful smile passed across his face.

"Nothing but a fairytale."

Chapter 5

The princess drifted back to her chambers like a bird with cracked wings, faltering every few steps and readjusting her gait. All sense of equilibrium had vanished the moment Asher said those final words. It was a miracle she'd even found her way back to the villa—

"Milady?"

She froze in the doorway of her bedroom, only to find someone was already inside.

It was a fae, that much was clear from a glance. The young woman was the kind of lovely that spoke to some higher power's blessing, rather than anything that could have come from this place. She had fair skin and rich, chestnut hair that flowed in gentle ripples to her waist. But it was pulled back efficiently and her gown was strikingly simple. She had also slipped in unannounced.

"Milady," the fae murmured again with a tiny smile. "That is how your people phrase these things, is it not? A title those who attend you must say?"

Evie stared in bewilderment, tears still drying on her face.

"I'm sorry," she finally managed. "Those who attend me—"

"My name is Leia. I have been assigned to your service for however long you choose to remain in Taviel. I've come to help prepare you for the gathering tonight." The fae looked the princess up and down, tilting her head with another curious smile. "I haven't spent much time amongst mortals. I'm still unsure how to address you..."

A rather pointed silence followed, and the princess suddenly remembered her query.

Milady.

"You don't...you don't have to say it," she stammered, trying to gather herself. The fae looked at her inquisitively, and she let out a little sigh. "Yes, that's what they call me."

Leia nodded soundly, as if the matter was settled. "Shall I draw you a bath then, milady? Or are you pressed for time?"

The princess cast a glance out the window, trying to gauge the position of the sun. The hours had gotten away from her in the quest to find Asher, but it had not yet touched the horizon.

"I'm not sure," she began uncertainly, still trying to compose herself. "We aren't set to meet until sometime this evening..."

The fae studied her carefully, those bright eyes lingering on the mud-stained shoes and tear-stained cheeks. Then she gestured to the adjoining room with a pleasant smile.

"There is time enough, I believe. And the water may do you good." She kept her arm raised, waiting for the princess to join her. "Come, I shall prepare it for you."

Evie hesitated a few seconds, but could see no alternative but to follow. As a people, the Fae were generally consistent in this regard—making gentle 'suggestions' for others to obey.

"I didn't know you were coming," she admitted as she followed Leia into the bath. "No one said I would be given a fae...attendant."

She caught herself swiftly, substituting another word at the last second. Somehow, she didn't think she could ever refer to the lovely immortal as a servant.

Leia smiled to herself, taking a towel down from the shelf. "You are to be given many, if you are to marry our prince. You may even be forced to learn *my* proper title, just as I have learned yours."

Evie flushed with a smile of her own, watching as the fae moved briskly around the tub.

She twisted a lever and flipped a dial, sweeping gracefully towards a row of slender shelves along the far wall. There were jars upon these shelves, full of petals and ointments and other things the princess had never really considered before that very moment.

Leia paused before them, tilting her head in quiet deliberation. Then she took a pinch of violet petals from a crystal basin and sprinkled them over the bath.

"This is asterlae," she said in a soft, melodious voice. "It soothes the muscles and calms the nerves." Her eyes flicked to the princess. "A suitable choice before meeting with a carionelle."

The smile faded and the princess flinched against the word.

"I suppose everyone is speaking of it," she said wearily, leaning against the side of the tub. A cloud of sweet-scented steam was drifting into the air. "It must have come as a shock."

The fae shrugged, kneeling down to finish her preparations.

"It is prudent, considering we are on the brink of war." She glanced again at the princess before rising gracefully to her feet. "Though prudence and love are rarely natural companions. I would imagine it was more of a shock to you, though the suggestion came from your own mouth."

Evie stared at her in surprise.

Never once had her childhood servants spoken in such a direct manner, yet nothing in the fae's words or disposition bore the slightest disrespect.

Because she's not a servant. She's an attendant.

"Is that what I should say to the carionelle?" she joked lightly, trying to ignore the rush of nerves that twisted her stomach. "That upon reflection, I desire something slightly less prudent?"

Fae were not often free with their emotions. At least not around those who didn't share their immortal blood. But this one seemed less inhibited than the rest. At any rate, she was kind.

Her lips curved with a touch of amusement.

"I expect the carionelle will do most of the talking."

The bath was ready and the princess disrobed quickly and stepped into the tub. The moment she did that warm fragrance seeped into her very bones, bringing a gasp of surprise to her lips.

"Oh...this is heaven."

The fae glanced back with another smile. "Asterlae."

I'll have to remember that...

For the next little while, the troubles of the world faded away as the princess surrendered herself to the irresistible power of those magic petals. Her mind quieted, her breathing slowed, and those hard knots that had twisted in her shoulders began to slowly ease away.

When the water finally began to cool she stood up again, only to have Leia immediately appear and drape a towel over her shoulders. A dress was waiting on the bed. One of the silken immortal gowns she had considered, then shied away from earlier that day.

Was that only this morning? It seems like a year has gone by.

"That's lovely," she said listlessly, watching as the fae picked it up.

"It was in your bureau," Leia answered, shaking it out with an appraising eye. "*Attendants* are allowed to search for such things, and I thought the color a compliment to you. Although I am fond of the green you were wearing earlier."

Evie glanced at her discarded dress, suppressing an involuntary shiver.

"Actually...I don't much care for that one anymore." She looked deliberately in the opposite direction, blinking tears from her eyes. "Dispose of it for me, will you?"

The fae stared at her a moment before bowing her head. "As you wish."

The clothes worn by the fair folk were easily as suited to angels—light as a feather, dusted with an ethereal shimmer, and surprisingly complicated. As the princess was quick to learn.

"How does this..."

Her fingers made tangles where none had existed before, muddling what had looked to be a simple process before Leia swiftly stepped in to help.

"Allow me, milady."

A few gentle touches and the dress unfurled to the floor, swishing around Evie's feet like the waves of a sunlit sea. She turned back and forth in front of the mirror, seeing past the dazzling exterior, pinching her bleached skin for a little color and practicing a formal smile.

"There...that looks appropriate, doesn't it?"

It hadn't struck her as a strange thing to say but the fae looked up quickly in the reflection, an uncertain expression on her face. She considered the princess a moment before answering.

"It may have been a prudent choice, milady...but there is a cost to such a thing. My people are in celebration, but there isn't a soul within the city gates who doesn't understand the sacrifice you are making. There isn't a soul who isn't grateful a hundred times in return."

She picked up the discarded gown on her way to the door.

"I'll put that green dress in the back of the bureau, if you ever decide to wear it again."

EVIE LINGERED FOR AS long as she could in her chambers, then began the slow march down the hall. Given the sensitive nature of what they were to be discussing, the notorious matchmaker had agreed to meet not within the citadel but at the villa itself. A table and chairs had been pulled under the shade trees in the center of the courtyard, just where Leonor had taken them a few hours before.

A few hours...will this day NEVER end?

She paused near the outer doors, lingering just out of sight.

She'd only met the man once, that fateful night when she received the prophecy, but his image had burned forever into her mind. Tall and thin, rigid and unsettling. With skin that crinkled like withered petals and a pair of clawed, grasping hands. They'd been introduced at a feast, but she hadn't seen him take a single bite. He'd stared at her and Ellanden instead, looking just as hungry.

Sure enough, he was sitting alone at the table—eating something that looked suspiciously like tiny fish. She stretched on her toes, trying to get a better look, when a movement caught her eye.

...Landi?

The prince had approached from the opposite entrance and was standing only a few feet away. He hadn't seen her yet, quite possibly because his eyes were closed tight. One hand was braced on a pillar for support, and he appeared to be muttering under his breath.

The princess froze—trapped between the fae and the fish.

She was about to sneak right back to her chambers under the guise of having forgotten something, when Ellanden opened his eyes suddenly and found himself looking straight at her.

"...hi."

She blurted it before she could stop herself then froze in the aftermath, wishing she'd kept her mouth shut. The fae had frozen as well, probably wondering how long she'd been standing there and if she'd seen the full extent of his psychological meltdown. It looked as though he was about to ask a probing question or two to that effect, when a sudden slurping sound echoed between them.

"What is that?"

She followed his gaze back to where Melkins was delightedly inhaling what seemed to be an entire school of fish. They hadn't been cooked, they hadn't been descaled. It looked as though they had simply gotten lost in the river and inexplicably found themselves on the man's plate.

Ellanden absentmindedly drifted closer, looking as though he might be sick.

"Does he even chew them?"

In their defense the friends sincerely tried to look away, but it was utterly useless. Instead, they watched in a kind of trance as the ageless matchmaker sucked down one tiny creature after other. When the final tail vanished down his throat, Ellanden turned away with a grimace.

"Well, it worked...I'm officially a vegetarian."

The princess flashed a weak grin. "Leonor will be thrilled."

The fae dined like the rest of his people when he was at Taviel, but it had always been to the councilman's chagrin that he ate differently when he was away. Evie remembered one argument in particular, when he'd returned from a summer spent at his grandmother's Kreo camp.

"What do you expect?" he'd cried after being chided for a throw-away line in a story. "They live in a desert, nothing else grows." When the elder refused to relent, he'd thrown up his hands in exasperation. "Would you have me starve?"

At that point, Evie had guessed it was an honest toss-up.

A door opened and closed behind them, startling her back to the present, and both friends turned to see their fathers walking together down the hall. Leonor himself was with them, wearing a look of strained patience, as if the three had already gone round for round.

Ellanden stiffened automatically, watching them approach.

"That's not the only thing that will thrill him," he muttered, throwing a glance over his shoulder at the courtyard. "What kind of name is *Melkins* anyway?"

Evie followed his gaze. "A stupid one."

They shared a quick look, then turned to greet their parents.

While Dylan was tense and grim, Cassiel seemed to have adopted a forced optimism since last they'd seen him. He nodded a greeting at Evie, then flashed his son a quick smile.

"I wasn't sure you were coming," he admitted, leaving the rest of them to wonder what would have happened if that was the case. "I thought we might need to organize a search."

Dylan shot him a look, but Leonor stepped forward with an approving smile.

"Of course he came," he interjected smoothly. "He understands what's at stake."

Cassiel clenched his jaw, but focused only on his son. "Nothing has been decided. This is a formality, nothing more. We will hear what the man has to say, then think on it. That is all."

Who are you trying to convince?

Ellanden opened his mouth to answer then closed it again, looking abruptly tired. Dylan clapped his shoulder before stepping past both of them towards his daughter.

"Are you sure about this?" he asked softly. "There are other things we can still try."

She tried to smile, squeezing his hands. "No, there aren't."

The men exchanged a nervous look, unable to dispute it. Then Leonor wisely ushered them forward, steering both children with a gentle hand. "Then let's see what he has to say..."

MELKINS GLANCED UP the moment the group entered the courtyard, pushing the empty platter towards the center of the table and pushing to his feet with an oily smile.

"Your Majesties!" He clapped his hands together, offering half a bow to the monarchs before turning in earnest to their children. "My dear girl, you grow more radiant by the day. And Your Grace," he inclined his head respectfully to Ellanden, "being home agrees with you."

The fae stood motionless in front of him then swept briskly to the opposite side of the table, settling himself in the farthest chair. Evie stared after him, forcing a smile in return.

"Thank you," she managed. "And thank you for agreeing to meet with us."

"It's my pleasure!" Melkins sank back into his seat with a wave of his hand as the others took their cue and arranged themselves around the table. "I was hoping to speak with you both much sooner, ten years sooner, in fact...but better late than never."

His eyes gleamed in the waning sunlight, reflecting the watery remains on his plate.

"I was actually a bit surprised to hear your announcement in the citadel," he confessed. "I wasn't aware such a decision had been made."

"You couldn't have been too surprised," Ellanden muttered just loud enough for the others to hear, "considering you were already in the city. And no decision has been made," he continued in a louder voice. "We are here only to listen."

The carionelle nodded slowly, never breaking his gaze.

It was a game they were playing. And while it might have been new to the children, it was a game he had played many times. In over a thousand years, he had never lost.

He had no intention of breaking that streak today.

"So you are to be the one," he murmured. "The one who needs convincing." Those thin lips twitched into a smile. "I should have known from the look on your face at the citadel. You didn't bolt for the exit, I'll give you that. But I've never seen someone look so pale."

The prince clenched his jaw, clutching the arms of his chair. "I'm glad this is such an amusement for you," he fired back. "It must be very easy to discuss such things when the consequences of such matters are never yours to bear."

Leonor leaned forward, holding up a hand. "Perhaps we should start by merely laying out the facts," he suggested soothingly.

Melkins inclined his head, eyes still locked on the prince.

"The matter is a simple one," he began abruptly. "With the blood in your veins, both you and the princess represent each of the four kingdoms. That is rare enough by itself, but in a stroke of good fortune you also happen to wear crowns. You will marry, and in doing so unite the realm."

There was a pang of silence, felt by everyone around the table.

"...and save it from destruction."

Five heads snapped up and turned to the princess at the same time. Her cheeks flamed, but she repeated the words, keeping her eyes on Melkins.

"We would unite the realm...and save it from destruction." She balled her hands into fists, keeping them tight in her lap. "That's the *entire* reason we would ever consider something like this."

The others remained silent, but the matchmaker smiled as if she'd said something quaint. Not for the first time she remembered that he'd been received at court even before they set out on the prophecy, long before any of them knew a thing about Kaleb Grey. The man played with kingdoms and crowns the way others played with cards, dancing those of noble birth across the board like a puppet-master. He must have thought it highly convenient when some dastardly enemy appeared and began to threaten them all—saved him a lot of time and scheming.

"Yes, of course," he answered with that same honeyed smile before turning back to the prince. "So you see, Your Grace, there is very little we must discuss—"

"'Very little we must discuss,'" Ellanden repeated slowly, his dark eyes ablaze. "I was told yesterday, in front of a room full of people, that I am to be married. I was informed of this. It was certainly news to me." He flashed a searing look at the princess. "So I apologize if I'm a little behind and you consider the conversation to be already finished, but *I'm not there yet*."

Instead of arguing the point, Melkins leaned back in his chair—regarding the fae with the hint of a smile. An old, brittle smile, like dried leaves crackling under the sun.

"You remind me of someone I knew long ago."

Evie glanced at him curiously.

"How quaint," Ellanden snapped, losing what little remained of his composure. "Let's all take a moment to drown in the nostalgia...no, wait...you're about to *ruin* my *life*!"

The others shared an anxious glance as Melkins chuckled under his breath.

"Yes, that's him."

Cassiel took his son's arm, murmuring something in his native tongue as Dylan ran a weary hand over his eyes. "This is going exactly as expected..."

"I do not seek to spoil anything for you, child." Melkins leaned forward once again, studying the young fae. "I'm merely giving you a chance—"

"You're just saying I can never be happy," Ellanden interrupted. "I should nod agreeably, keep my silence, and resign myself to the fact that in my whole life I can never be happy."

Evie stared mutely across the table, feeling as though a light had gone out.

Is that really how he feels? That we could never find a way to be happy?

"I don't know why you think that's your right," Melkins countered in frustration. "You were born a prince. You were born to a life of public service. By its very definition, that means putting the well-being of your people above that of yourself. You have no expectation to happiness. That is a privilege. One that's afforded to many people before it can be afforded to you—"

There was a sudden *bang* as a knife buried itself in the table, sending a spider-web of cracks through the ancient stone. Evie jumped a mile, then looked in shocked silence at her uncle.

"Careful, matchmaker," he said casually, tracing the edges of the blade. "Time may not have found a way to kill you, but I'm willing to get creative..."

Leonor hissed something under his breath, but Cassiel kept his dark eyes fixed upon the carionelle. When the man finally met his gaze, they cooled with a chilling smile.

"I understand my responsibility to the people," Ellanden inserted quietly, steering them back on course, "but I speak not only for myself. You are telling me to destroy not just my own life but the lives of three others. Am I to answer for all of them? Are we to decide their future right now?"

"Do you want to play numbers, Ellanden?" Leonor asked calmly. "Because that is not a game you would win."

Another silence fell over the table as everyone looked in opposite directions. Some were staring at the ivory rooftops of the city, others were staring at the jagged cracks in the stone.

"Do you not love the princess?" Melkins prompted gently, tempered by the appearance of a blade. "Do you not care for her deeply as a friend? Do you not love your people just as deeply?"

Ellanden shifted uncomfortably, as if it was suddenly difficult to breathe. "Yes, of course I do. But—"

"You have seen the darkness racing towards them. The Fates themselves have commanded you to intervene. Do you not wish to do all in your power to protect them? Especially after..."

He didn't finish. He didn't have to.

Especially after leaving them alone for ten years.

The fae stared back in silence.

It was a terrible card, played at exactly the right moment. He wanted to argue, he wanted to scream. But his ears were already full of screams, and all the fight suddenly went out of him.

He hesitated a moment longer, then bowed his head.

"How would we...how would we even go about it?"

An invisible weight dropped onto the table, crushing everyone sitting alongside. Leonor was pleased but saddened, while their fathers leaned back with matching sighs. Evie suddenly realized she couldn't bear to watch it happen. She stared instead at the falls, taking those measured breaths, wishing they were back in the woods and doing whatever she could not to openly cry.

Only Melkins was oblivious, leaning forward with an encouraging smile.

"Which part troubles you?"

Judging from the fae's face, he was 'troubled' by the entire arrangement. But he latched onto the most innocuous question, a logistical one, to ease them in.

"There are four kingdoms," he answered, "and only two of us. Where would we even live?"

"An excellent question, Your Grace." Melkins folded his hands on the table, oblivious to the sudden despondence. "And one that provides you some options. While the ceremony itself should take place as quickly as possible, there is no reason why you and the princess cannot live in separate residences in the months that follow. Of course, you'll need to be together on formal occasions, but until the arrival of your children there is much that can be—"

"What?"

Ellanden lifted his head, staring at the man in a daze.

Since the sun had risen the previous morning, he had considered this newfound crisis from every possible angle. He'd worn a trail in the center of his room, pacing in angry circles, playing out a thousand different arguments. But a rather obvious component had completely slipped his mind.

We are expected to have a child.

Cassiel took one look at his face, then lifted a hand for silence.

"That's enough," he commanded under his breath. "We can continue this tomorrow."

"But we are nearly finished," Melkins continued obliviously, pleased to have reached an accord. "Your children will live separately from you some of the time, unless you and Everly—"

Ellanden stood up and left the courtyard.

The others stared after him in silence, unable to move from their chairs. As if to mock them a few of those tiny songbirds perched upon the railing, chirping happily back and forth. They could have stayed like that forever if Cassiel had not turned slowly to the carionelle—a look of pure, savage, hatred stirring in his eyes. For a split second, the princess thought he might actually stab the man.

Melkins apparently thought so, too, because he was the first to speak.

"I know what you wish to say, but with all due respect, my lord, you have no more cards to play when it comes to placing the good of your child above the good of the realm."

Evie sucked in a quick breath. Dylan half-rose to his feet, ready to intervene.

But Cassiel merely yanked his dagger from the table and vanished after his son. Leonor was soon to follow, glancing quickly at the rest of them before disappearing into the villa.

And then there were three...

"That was poorly handled," Dylan said quietly, throwing a hard look at Melkins. "And for all the gold in the realm, I would not have made an enemy of that particular man."

Evie looked nervously between them, but the matchmaker was strangely unfazed.

"Save your breath, Your Majesty." He leaned back in his chair, looking abruptly tired. "There is a reason that eons ago I was selected to perform this specific task, and the reason is that all parties involved—including yourself—cannot be impartial. If Katerina had been a commoner and the two of you had fallen in love, you could not have married her. You know that just as well as I."

Evie looked between them in shock, unable to believe he would speak so freely. But perhaps the same rules did not apply to such a man. At any rate, her mother had once confessed the same thing—how conflicted she'd been before Dylan had decided to take up his crown. Until he did, there was no way for them to be together. A princess had to marry a prince.

"Even then, you were pushing it," Melkins was saying. "I still maintain that the Queen of the High Kingdom would have done much better to have married a fae…but I suppose it turned out all right in the end."

Dylan raised his eyebrows slowly.

"*All right?*" he quipped. "You mean when we executed Nathaniel Fell and pulled the realm from the brink of annihilation? Yes, I suppose we did all right."

Melkins ignored this, wondering vaguely if there were any more fish. "It does not change the facts. Between the two of them, your daughter and Cassiel's son represent each of the four kingdoms. It is a match made in heaven."

Four kingdoms brought together under a single banner.

Four kingdoms united under a single crown.

"But there are five kingdoms," Evie said quietly.

Both men turned to look at her in surprise. She had been almost completely silent during the entire meeting. Her father had half-believed her incapable of speech.

She blushed under their shared gaze, but repeated the point again. "There are five kingdoms. You forgot the vampires."

Melkins softened with a touch of genuine sympathy. "The vampires are not a kingdom, and your friend Asher is not a prince. I'm sorry, my dear, but you should know, historically speaking, this is one of the best outcomes you could hope for."

She honestly couldn't tell if he was joking. "…how do you figure?"

He leaned back again in his chair, considering it himself. "You know him—most people didn't. You're not related—that was a dark era. What's more, you actually *like* him. You're friends. My darling girl…that's the dream."

The dream.

Perhaps it was the look that Dylan gave him, perhaps it was the expression on the princess' face, but the old man wisely gathered up his papers and departed as well.

"Believe it or not, that was a productive first meeting," he called over his shoulder. "And you should be proud of what you did in the citadel, Your Highness. This land owes you a great debt."

Then there were two...

Dylan and Evie stared after the carionelle for a long time after he left. Long enough that the waning sun began to flicker and evening shadows rolled in across the sky.

When he finally opened his mouth, she silenced him with a tight smile. The very same smile she'd been practicing in the mirror. He hesitated a moment, then pressed a kiss to her cheek.

"I wish there was another way."

She nodded quickly, then left the table behind—walking up the hallway as quickly as she could without breaking into a run. She made it all the way back to her room before she started to cry.

Chapter 6

The day may technically have been governed by the rising and falling of the sun, but this one had defied all earthly physics. Not since she was trapped in the sorcerer's cave had Evie felt herself in the grips of such an unending purgatory—as if time itself had stalled out of spite.

So she shouldn't have been surprised when the night had one twist left in store.

"You're back early," Cosette looked up with a start, perched with her boyfriend on the edge of the princess' bed. "We were prepared to make a night of it."

Evie paused in the doorway, staring over the little scene.

The fae and the shifter had apparently forsaken the public dining hall and smuggled up their dinner directly from the kitchens. The silken blanket was laden with breads, cheese and pastries, while Seth was using what the princess recognized to be her own pillow to balance his plate.

He removed it slowly, tossing it back on the bed. "...how was it?"

Her smiled faded as she leaned against the door.

Such a familiar scene, but the numbers were wrong. Only two, when there should have been five waiting to see her. The kingdoms were aligning but their fellowship had broken, drawing some of them together while the others were scattered in the wind.

"Evie?" Seth tilted his head to catch her gaze, asking the question again. "How did it go?"

She blinked quickly, closing the door behind her.

"Please, let's not talk about it." She settled on the blanket between them, unable to remember the last time she'd had something to eat. "Tell me what you thought of Gran."

Normally, they would have pressed. But something in the princess' expression required caution. At any rate, it happened to have been the *perfect* thing to say.

Cosette's eyes danced with a sudden smile, while Seth blushed a million shades of red.

"...she invited me to tea."

And he had clearly never been more disconcerted in his life. Evie studied him a moment, smearing honey onto a biscuit, before going out on a limb.

"Is that a euphemism—"

"It's just tea," Cosette interrupted swiftly, reassuring him. "And you won't be faced with it alone. I'll go with you. To bear witness—if nothing else."

Another commonality about the Fae: they were never as comforting as they thought.

Seth flashed the woodland princess a look, while Evie laughed in spite of herself.

It was easy to pretend that things were normal when it was just the three of them, sharing an evening meal. Almost as if they were back in the forest, trudging along on their epic misadventure yet inexplicably happy. While the problems of the rest of the world seemed distant and faded away.

"She truly isn't that bad once you get to know her," Evie reassured him. "Sort of an acquired taste. Although, given the hallucinogenic properties of some Kreo herbs, I'd be careful of the tea."

"She's talking about Gran," Cosette clarified. "*Not* me."

Seth chuckled to himself, wrapping an arm around the fae's waist. "I knew a man once—a drunk, who lived for some time in our village. Each night he would let the drink take him, and when he was quite beside himself he'd roam the streets until sunrise, singing nursery rhymes and bellowing at the stars. People were afraid of him. For a time, I was afraid of him myself. But after some weeks had passed, I found myself whistling along."

The shifter's eyes warmed with a nostalgic smile.

"Gran reminds me of this man."

...that's fair.

"What happened to him?" Evie asked curiously.

"He drank five pints of ale in one night and wandered over the falls. We found his body washed ashore a week later. Some say the flagon was still clasped in his hand."

The princess wasn't sure of this last part, but it made for a good story.

With lingering smiles the friends fell into a comfortable silence, passing around a bottle of cider as they filled their stomachs with food. Considering how the day had started, it wasn't a terrible way to end. But of course, there was only so long such a silence could last.

"Evie...how was it?"

The princess set down her glass with a sigh, glancing up to see both Cosette and Seth staring at her with the same frozen expression. The fae had held back the question as long as possible, but the candles were burning low, her family was divided, and a new dawn was just a few hours away.

"I think it's going to happen," Evie murmured in a low voice. "I think we're going to go through with it."

Such a thing hadn't been explicitly said...but she had proposed the idea and Ellanden had surrendered. Given the circumstances, she didn't see much better confirmation than that.

A mix of emotions chased themselves through Cosette's dark eyes, flying one after the next. Then she turned to the window, looking remarkably flat.

"Then I guess we're saved," she said dully.

I guess so.

THE PRINCESS SLEPT poorly that night, tossing and turning with dreams of shrieking songbirds and decapitated fish. But she awoke fresh the next morning, with a new purpose.

We have made the decision. Now it's time to make peace.

She leapt from her bed and dressed quickly, forcing a comb through her tangled locks while stuffing her feet into a random pair of shoes. It wouldn't occur to her until later that Leia would soon have come to assist with every step. She was too consumed with the present task.

The night may not have provided rest, but it did provide some clarity.

She did not accept that, inescapable as their situation was, it couldn't be maneuvered in such a way to make it more bearable. She did not accept that they had surrendered any chance of happiness, as Ellanden seemed to think. There was a third option, a sliver of precious middle ground.

We just have to find it.

The second she set foot in the hall, she set out for the northernmost part of the villa. It may have been a sprawling series of rooms, but either by coincidence or careful design the chambers of all the fae had been situated together in the loveliest section, by the gardens and the misting falls.

She darted through the corridors quickly, not wanting to run into anyone else by mistake, then paused automatically when she came to Ellanden's door.

Knock...then duck. In case he's armed.

It was a ritual she'd practiced many times since childhood, oftentimes saving herself from a nasty wound. Despite his natural alignment with the sun and the stars, the woodland prince was notoriously difficult in the mornings. Perhaps it was his Kreo blood, or mere adolescent sloth.

"Landi?"

She knocked quickly, then crouched to the floor—waiting for the telltale swish of arrows or the sharp crack of a blade. When neither happened, she straightened up slowly.

"Are you in there?"

Silence.

She waited another moment, ear pressed to the door, then wandered at a slower pace across the hallway to his parents' chambers. There were people inside, she could hear them through the door. Strange voices, speaking in a strange cadence. She paused outside, staring with a faint frown.

Just knock. What's the worst that could happen?

Perhaps it was tempting fate, but no sooner had she lifted a fist than the door opened by itself and Cassiel slipped into the hall. He didn't immediately see her, though she was standing right in front of him. He seemed far more preoccupied with the people he'd just left.

"Good morning."

The fae jumped in surprise, staring down at his adoptive niece. Only then did she realize he'd been holding a blade. He slipped it quickly into its sheath.

"Good morning, sweetheart. You're up early."

She nodded swiftly, feeling a little nervous. "Is Ellanden here?"

Her uncle opened his mouth to answer, then the voices in the bedroom rose to sudden new heights. Swelling with tension and speed, clipping themselves short into odd patterns of rhyme, so that Evie abruptly recognized them as more than just a chant, but some kind of incantation.

Tanya...Gran...

The second her ears cut through the magic she was able to pick out the individual voices of the Kreo elder and their shape-shifting queen. They dipped in and out like tightly wound spirals, so that even on the other side of the doorway the princess felt a tension pulling her towards the room.

"What are they doing?" she asked quietly, grateful she was standing outside.

Cassiel glanced back towards the door, looking unexpectedly sad. "They're trying to resurrect the sorcerer who held you prisoner."

Evie's pulse spiked with a sudden jolt. "Why?!"

The fae turned back to face her. "So we can kill him all over again."

It was an utterly outrageous idea, but at the same time a part of the princess wasn't really surprised. Their parents weren't the type to forgive easily, let alone someone who'd actually done them harm. In the sorcerer's case, it seemed death itself was too easy a punishment. The man had kept their children prisoner for ten years. They wanted a turn with him themselves.

It wasn't surprising, but the princess was terrified all the same.

"...will that work?"

An image of that cobwebbed face drifted through her mind, and she didn't care how many armies were beside her—she wanted to run screaming right out of the house.

"No," Cassiel said softly, "it won't work."

Of course not. If there was a chance, he'd be on the other side of the door.

Evie nodded quickly, realizing that Ellanden would surely have fled the room himself. She tentatively lifted her eyes to her uncle, battling an unexpected wave of nerves at the same time.

Good morning, sweetheart.

It hadn't struck her until that very moment that she was surprised to hear him say it. The Lord of the Fae hadn't said more than a few words since she'd proposed to his only son. The most he'd done was throw her a tight smile before threatening the man in charge of marrying them with a blade.

"What is it?" he asked curiously, noting her change in expression.

She blushed, tucking her hair behind her ears. "...I thought you hated me."

His face lightened with a look of surprise. "*Hated* you? Surely you jest—"

"I did this," she interrupted quietly, gesturing back to the courtyard. "In the citadel...I'm the one who spoke out and set this plan into motion. Whatever hurt Ellanden is feeling, it's my fault."

"You merely gave voice to what a hundred other people were already saying behind closed doors," he replied gently. "There was a reason the carionelle was already in the city. In times of peril, such an alliance is an obvious solution. And while it pains me to say it, given the bloodlines that run through our kingdoms, you and Ellanden are an obvious match."

"But it pains you," she echoed, tear prickling her eyes. "You just said it yourself. You were ready to chop that man to pieces yesterday, just because he threatened your son's happiness—"

"I have lost reason when it comes to Ellanden," Cassiel admitted, echoing the same words that had been hurled back at him by a dozen worried friends. "This new heartbreak has come too soon on the heels of his return. I would keep him locked in a velvet box until this is all over." His dark eyes tightened with the hint of a frown. "But none of that has anything to do with you."

Those tears swelled, but she bit down on her lip—refusing to allow herself to cry.

The fae had always inspired frank and genuine discussions, but that was the problem. She didn't want to be honest. Because she couldn't stand to cause him even the slightest bit more pain.

He stared at her a few seconds longer, then leaned back with a touch of surprise.

"...Katerina told you of the woods."

Their eyes locked for a suspended moment, then he wrapped an arm around her shoulder and led her silently away from the door. The incantations faded to a distant memory as they stepped out of the villa and into the soft glow of a vibrant new dawn. It washed over them, stilling all other thoughts and contemplations as they walked in silence to the balcony, gazing over the side.

"I couldn't believe when she told me," Evie finally murmured, dabbing her eyes. "You loved him so much that you actually…" She cut herself short, unable to continue. "And then I stand up in front of everyone and ruin his life—"

"There was no love in what I did," Cassiel interrupted in a quiet voice. "There was only grief. Only those who have lost all semblance of hope find themselves journeying to those woods."

It was quiet for a while between them. Nothing but the distant call of birds ringing over the falls. Then all at once Cassiel turned towards her, those dark eyes glowing with new light.

"But my hope has returned. My *child* has returned. Those woods are finished for me." He bent his head lower, catching her eye. "And nothing you've done could drive me back there again."

She nodded dismissively, but he squeezed her hand.

"You mustn't worry, my dearest. And you mustn't lose faith. For as bleak as it may seem, there is hope in this union as well. The future is not fixed… there's no telling what time may reveal."

Her eyebrows rose in surprise. "You think we should go through with it?"

He paused, considering his reply. "No, I don't."

She nodded to herself, looking back over the falls. "*You* certainly didn't. You refused such a match. You refused to marry my mother." She hesitated, then cast him a sideways glance. "But if the realm had required it…would you have wed?"

He considered again, lips twitching in a faint smile. "Fortunately, a higher power saw fit to freeze everyone pressuring us in a dark enchantment tied to a wizard's spell. I don't think we'll be so fortunate for that to happen twice."

She laughed in spite of herself. "No, probably not."

They were quiet for a while longer, listening to that echoing song.

Since taking off on the wings of a dragon and reuniting with her family, the princess hadn't found many moments of such tranquility. There was always a tension, or an implication, or a vague anxiety tugging at the corners of her heart. But it was hard to feel those things now. The Ivory City had a way of washing such feelings away, a way of leaving one feeling renewed and clean.

Cassiel looked out at his kingdom, then turned back to the girl at his side. "Everly...you must stop blaming yourself for doing what is required. Of everyone here, you were selected to receive the prophecy. There is no blame in that. There is only courage."

Her body quaked with a quiet sob and he pulled her into an embrace.

"And I could never hate you," he murmured, resting his cheek on her hair. "I could hate your mother. I frequently hate your father. But I could never hate you." He pressed a kiss to her forehead, pulling back with a tender smile. "I would lock you in that box as well."

She smiled tearfully in return, wiping her eyes and pushing back her hair. "*Ellanden* hates me."

Cassiel laughed under his breath. "He might, a little. But that will fade in time."

She glanced up in surprise. "Are you saying he'll come round to the idea?"

He laughed again, picturing that look of stubborn defiance in his son's eyes. "I'm saying he's your dearest friend, and could never hate you for long."

She considered this in silence, wishing she'd been more careful with her words. She'd asked her uncle if they should go through with the wedding. She hadn't asked if he thought they *needed* to.

Before she rephrase it, a door opened behind them and the sound of light footsteps echoed down the hall. Cassiel glanced over his shoulder before turning back to the falls with a wry smile.

"Speak of the devil..."

"*There* you are!" Dylan swept angrily into the courtyard, waving a sheet paper in his hand. He paused just long enough to give his daughter a kiss before slapping it into the fae's chest. "I have received *five* separate messages from that wretched matchmaker, chiding the two of us for 'conduct unbecoming the lords of the land.' Can you believe that? He actually sent me a note!"

Cassiel read it quickly, unable to suppress a smile. "It's addressed to you," he remarked. "It doesn't mention me anywhere—"

"You're implied," Dylan interrupted, snatching it back. "I swear, we should have had that man drawn and quartered the moment we met. Conduct unbecoming..." He trailed off with an almost vampiric hiss. "It's incredible no one's taken the time to burn him at the stake!"

Cassiel's eyes danced with sarcasm. "You've seen him. Maybe they have."

Evie stared towards the villa as they continued bantering back and forth behind her, the fae's earlier words echoing in her ears. *I'm saying he's your dearest friend, and could never hate you for long.*

"I have an errand," she said without preamble, heading towards the steps. "I'll see you both for the evening meal. Don't incinerate anyone while I'm gone."

Her father muttered something that sounded suspiciously like "*no promises*", rereading the note with a vicious gleam, but she was already down the steps and moving towards the pavilion.

SINCE HER ANNOUNCEMENT in the citadel, the streets were teeming with new energy. Leia had said her people were in celebration, but what the princess witnessed went a bit beyond all that.

It was as though the city itself had been brought back to life.

Gone was the unnatural silence that had plagued the bustling markets, gone was the layer of tension that framed every conversation and haunted every laugh. Cassiel had been wise to recognize the transformation from high atop the mountain, but it sank into every level of the city beneath.

Hope.

"Good morning, Your highness!"

Evie whirled about in surprise as a pair of people she'd never seen waved to her from across the pavilion, delivering a basket of freshly-baked bread. A member of the High Council was soon to follow, inclining his head with a radiant smile as he whisked from one meeting to the next.

There was a momentum that had been lacking before. A forward propulsion that broke free of the resignation and grey doldrums that had troubled the city before.

There was a purpose now. There was a chance.

And it all started with a ring.

A row of shops caught Evie's eye and she paused in spite of herself, staring through the glass at a brilliant display of gemstones sprinkled like dew across a silken sheet. Tear-drop pendants of silver-dusted ivory, intricately woven bracelets of some pale translucent stone. No matter which way they were facing, every miniscule facet seemed to catch the light, glowing like tiny beacons. Each one so exquisitely radiant, she half-believed they'd serve as torches if placed in the dark.

Her eyes came to rest upon the selection of rings at the very top—glittering across the silken sheet like a sudden spattering of stars. A sudden chill swept over her and she took a step closer.

Would Ellanden give me something like this? Or would I have something more ceremonial to wear?

A part of her still couldn't believe she was thinking it. Just a few days ago, her course had been set. She had fallen in love for the very first time. The kind of love that was eternal. The kind of love that drove all others to shame. Now here she was...contemplating marriage to someone else.

That stubborn, defiant part had been broken and chided—but it was still screaming. Looking at all those lovely rings, sparkling innocently in the sun, she didn't think it would ever stop.

"Would you like to see them, milady?"

She jumped a mile as a woman's face appeared above the gems. She was speaking from inside but the door was open, so the princess could hear her quite easily. A coaxing smile lifted the corners of her mouth as she gestured again to the rings, lifting them higher for a better look.

"It never hurts to look."

Rather fanciful language for a fae, but in this case the woman was wrong. It most certainly *did* hurt to look. It hurt just thinking about it.

"No...thank you."

Evie backed away as though she'd been burned, hurrying quickly across the remainder of the pavilion, then vanishing once more down the stairs that spiraled beneath the citadel floor.

She didn't need a ring. She needed a drink.

Chapter 7

When Evie and Asher were both six years old, Ellanden had convinced them it would be a good idea to take up drinking as a full-time pursuit. While Asher amusedly abstained, she had agreed whole-heartedly, not having the faintest idea what he was implying, and followed with the wide-eyed innocence of a child as the little fae stole a torch off the wall and snuck them down to the cellars.

Never before had she seen such a thing—she didn't even know it had existed. But in the early creation of that mystical city, one of the architects (perhaps out of a deep-seeded knowledge of his people, or perhaps with a bit too much time on his hands) had decided to hollow out a portion of the mountain to fill with spirits and wine. It was kept locked at all times, but such a thing had never stopped the young prince before. He reached into his robes, gleefully extracting the key.

"I swiped it when they were forcing me into the bath," he'd confided in a whisper, reaching above his head to stuff it into the lock. "No one ever frisks royalty."

The vampire and princess considered these words with a contemplative frown as the door swung open and he strutted inside with a magnanimous wave of his hands.

"Behold...our kingdom."

At that point, the princess took a delicate sniff and realized what the fae had meant when he said they'd *drink*. Her heart pounded and her eyes grew wide as the moon as the vampire gave the fae a boost and he took hold of the nearest bottle, dragging it out of sight behind a massive barrel of ale.

"I'm not sure how to get it open..." he murmured, running his fingers over the cork as the others crouched beside him. After a second he passed it to the vampire, who ripped it out with a pair of tiny fangs.

"*Brilliant,*" he grinned from ear to ear, "I knew you had those things for a reason!"

Considering they were the pint-size offspring of the realm's greatest heroes, they couldn't attempt such a thing without a bit of ceremony and flair. Ellanden lifted the bottle high above his head, demanding the nature spirits bless their first endeavor, while the princess crossed herself with a gesture she'd seen in the village chapel then spat impressively on the ground.

They'd shared about half a glass between them.

Then they'd passed out on the cellar floor.

But we're much older and wiser now...

An instinctual shiver crept up the princess' spine as she trotted down the last of the steps and peered cautiously into the shadowy hallway. Technically, there was nothing to fear. Technically, she could have simply asked Leia to bring a bottle of anything she liked up to her bedroom. But there was something about this particular errand she had to do by herself. And those technicalities did nothing to erase to decade of fear inspired by her parents' reaction to that very childhood story.

"Hello?"

There wasn't any answer, although the sound of distant voices echoed up the hall. The ancient cellar wasn't the only thing tucked away so deep in the mountain. The royal armory was situated just across the hall. Not until that very moment did she find the proximity strange.

Or convenient? Perhaps one effectively lubricates the other.

The farther she wandered down the corridor, the louder the voices grew. They were brisk yet cheerful, an echo of what she'd seen in the market above. No longer were the people of Taviel stuck in a holding pattern. An accord had been reached, and their enemy had been given a name.

It was a city in preparation.

The scent of whiskey and mulled spices drifted through the cellar door, but she paused in the center of the hall, peering towards the armory instead. While most warriors of the Fae preferred to train in the open air, there were several testing out the equipment and sparring playfully on the side. *Playfully* being a relative term, given the skillsets involved. After only a few seconds she found herself rooted breathlessly to the floor, watching in astonishment with fingers cupped over her mouth.

How do they move like that? she wondered, drifting a step closer. *What must it have been like the first time they ever tried?*

She could only imagine it must have been terrifying. She could only imagine the close proximity to a kingdom's worth of whiskey must have helped.

To most people, the limited space would have been a problem. But the group of fae she was watching paid little attention to such confinement and simply did as they pleased. When there wasn't enough room on the ground, they vaulted off the ceiling. When the ceiling grew tiresome they flew onto the shelving halfway in between, creating a multi-tiered attack that left Evie dizzy just watching.

Who precisely they were fighting remained a mystery.

About half a dozen were flying around the chamber in a fantastical spiral of blades and robes, colliding with violent regularity, but it seemed to be every man for himself.

And every woman.

Evie watched in astonishment as one of the warriors perched suddenly upon a rack of spears, slowing down enough that the princess could see the tumble of midnight tresses braided down her back. A silver-tipped arrow sliced through the air towards her face but she caught it with an easy flick of her fingers, twirling it back towards her attacker and throwing it with her bare hands.

Laughter rang out in sudden bursts, punctuated with a metallic clash of blades. Every so often, they'd venture too close to a group of officers conferring in the center and get batted away with an indulgent grin. Yes, it was lighthearted enough that the princess could only call it play.

But if one were to lose focus for even an instant...that *play* might cost them a hand.

She was still watching when one of the warriors detached himself suddenly from the game, lifting a hand in farewell before striding gracefully towards the door. The direction was obvious, but she was still in such a trance she didn't think to move and it almost struck her in the face.

"I'm sorry," he exclaimed immediately, closing it quickly behind him. "Why didn't—"

They froze at the same time, staring at each other in surprise.

It was the same fae from the dining hall. The one who'd knocked into her shoulder, called her a traitor, then stormed right out the door. She'd only glimpsed him for a moment, but needless to say his face had earned itself a permanent place in her mind. Fair skin, jet black hair, and eyes the color of spring leaves when the sunlight struck them from the other side.

He was startlingly beautiful, just like the rest of his people. He was also clearly dismayed the fates had seen fit to throw them together a second time.

He froze a second longer, then sank into a respectful bow.

"...Your Highness."

It took her a moment to catch her breath. Another moment to recover that Damaris pride.

"It's Jaziere, isn't it?" she said with a sneer, deliberately mispronouncing it. She remembered Ellanden angrily calling his name before he stormed out of the hall. "You left so quickly the last time, we were never properly introduced."

He kept his head bowed and didn't correct her.

"I apologize again, milady." His vibrant green eyes locked on the stone just ahead of her shoes. "That night is a point of shame for me. I'm afraid I had lost myself to drink—"

"—and felt free to speak your mind," she finished sharply, looking him up and down.

Under most circumstances she would have been far too embarrassed to have brought it up, but that night was a point of shame for her as well. Never had she been so publicly disrespected in her life—discounting the antics of her dearest friends—and she'd never understood why such a thing had gone unpunished. Especially considering the people dining with her in the room.

"Tegalin, right?" she quoted his own insult back to him. "You think I'm a traitor?"

His body tensed as his eyes flickered to the door behind him. She couldn't tell if he was praying they wouldn't be interrupted, or if he was dying for someone else to come out. When nothing happened he straightened up slowly, lifting his gaze to her face.

"No, milady," he said softly. "I don't think you're a traitor."

Not anymore.

She stared back in sudden, awkward silence—wishing she'd crumbled behind the door and let him be on his way. He was about a foot taller than she was, bedecked in armor, so instead of holding his gaze she stared at that instead. After just a second, her eyebrows rose in surprise.

"You're a captain."

To her astonishment, he actually blushed—dropping his gaze to the floor.

"Yes, Your Highness. Just...just recently promoted."

Her eyes narrowed with sudden suspicion. "How recently?"

He laughed softly, but kept his gaze down. "Not for that. Such disrespect would never be rewarded. I was surprised not to have been whipped."

Me, too.

She folded her arms and shifted her balance, intrigued by the man in spite of herself. "So you're a captain, but they still let you play around with the troops?"

He followed her glance back towards the armory before brightening with a true smile.

"It's how we learn. I still have much to learn. But I appreciate the opportunity to teach as well. If there is war on the horizon, I would like to be useful where I can."

Another surprising answer. She cast a secret look at his face before they both watched through the armory window as that same group of warriors flew faster and faster around the room.

The girl with the dark hair was particularly skilled. The princess watched with open amazement as she looped the people meant to be chasing her, and came down on the other side.

"She's incredible."

"My sister," Jaziere answered with a touch of pride. "Valeria."

She smiled in spite of herself, reminded suddenly of the way Cassiel sometimes looked at his own younger sister—openly affectionate the moment her eyes were somewhere else.

"Is she a captain, too?"

"She could be," he replied swiftly. "She has more talent than almost anyone here, including myself. But she has higher aspirations. She hopes to train her way into the king's guard."

Evie glanced at him in surprise before turning back to the girl.

She knew such positions were considered a great honor, awarded to those with unparalleled talent who had inevitably distinguished themselves in some way. But you would be hard pressed to find a fae without unparalleled talent. A level of experience was required as well. Most of those who served in the king's guard now were thousands of years old. Older than Cassiel was himself.

"She's very young," she murmured, almost to herself. "At least...she *looks* very young."

In the land of immortality, appearances were often deceiving.

"She's very gifted," Jaziere corrected sharply before catching himself. "At any rate, she has time enough for training. The gods willing, our young prince may never become king."

Evie nodded along, then went suddenly still.

The *king's* guard.

She had automatically assumed the male was speaking of her uncle, but upon reflection that didn't make sense. There were always twelve warriors charged with protecting the Lord and Lady of the Fae. Each of those positions had been long since filled.

This young captain was speaking of Ellanden. His sister was training to protect Ellanden.

On the fateful chance that immortality fell short, turning their prince into a king.

She turned away suddenly, unable to think of it, but the rules of decorum had fallen away and Jaziere was staring deep into her eyes.

"I was there in the citadel," he said quietly. "I heard what you said. Forgive me a further impertinence, milady...but such a sacrifice should not go unnoticed. It is not unnoticed by me."

A flaming blush burned the princess' cheeks and she nodded quickly to change the subject, turning her eyes once more to the silver armor stretched across his chest.

Like most things belonging to the Fae, even the tools they used for killing had been touched with a kind of grace. Swords were featherlight, bows curved into silver crescents. The metal itself they wore into battle had been designed to tell a tale. Their people valued crests and sigils. Most of them had light etchings in their armor—to identify lost souls and bring honor to the family name.

Ellanden never wore such things. She guessed he just assumed everyone would know who he was. But she was surprised to see that she recognized a talisman on her new friend.

"Narsi," she murmured with a faint smile. "Most of the families I know lay some claim to the heron...but your family has chosen hope." She reached without thinking to trace the trio of little birds—each one shaded slightly differently than the last. *Three.* "Do you have another sibling?"

For a brief moment, he went perfectly still.

"A brother...Orion. He was at Cadarest."

A sudden chill swept over her as Leonor's words echoed in her mind.

Cadarest was sacked.

She understood now why no one had reprimanded him back in the dining hall, why even her dutiful protectors had allowed him to walk away.

"I'm sorry," she murmured, lowering her eyes.

The fae nodded stiffly, suddenly eager to be on his way.

She stepped aside to let him pass, and the two of them headed in separate directions. He was off to a training arena on the other side of the forest, while she slipped secretly to the cellars. But neither of them was aware when they came to a simultaneous pause on opposite ends of the hall.

They listened for a moment to the sounds coming from the armory. The bursts of laughter and the clash of swords. They thought for a moment on all they had already sacrificed, on all that was yet to come. Then they considered their strange conversation and set off walking once more.

Feeling a little better about their chances.

WHEN EVIE KNOCKED AGAIN on Ellanden's door, she was armed with a weapon of her own. A bottle of aged Tarmini whiskey that some greedy servant had tried to hide on the topmost shelf.

He clearly wasn't expecting her, because he cracked open the door.

"I come bearing gifts."

His face hardened and he moved to slam it shut, when the label on the bottle—tilted towards him strategically—caught his eye. He deliberated a moment, then reached out to take it regardless. She held on to it tightly, wedging her foot in the door.

"I come with the bottle."

He hesitated a moment longer, then opened it with a sigh.

Victory!

She slipped inside before he could change his mind, closing the door behind her. It had been a long-shot, gaining entry this way. Her other plans had included the window and a stray cat.

"What do you want, Everly?"

He'd been calling her that more and more lately. Something formal. As if their childhood affections were finished and nicknames no longer applied.

She froze a split second, then gestured to the bottle. "I want to drink it."

He was turned away from her, facing deliberately towards the window, but she heard the sarcasm clearly in his voice. "...it's sunrise."

There was a beat.

"Do you care?"

He popped the lid off the bottle and looked around for glasses. The tray of untouched food beside his bed had already been removed by a servant. There was nothing left but a pitcher of water.

"I haven't any—"

The princess came up behind him and took a swig from the bottle, pressing it back into his hands. He stared at her a second, then did the same. Together they abandoned the furniture, sinking down onto the floor beside his bed and leaning against the mattress, passing the bottle between them.

In a disturbingly short amount of time, it was already half-gone.

It hit them both at the same time, catching them by surprise. Ellanden lifted the drink again to his lips, then lowered it without partaking—squinting slightly as he tried to read the label.

"This is...*incredibly* strong."

Evie bowed her head with a grin, glad he'd been the first to say it. "Yeah, I didn't really think it through."

He snorted with laughter, muttering under his breath, "What a novelty for you."

Shit.

"The concept of impulsivity."

Right.

"What a strange new feeling."

Okay.

He grabbed a pillow off the bed and swung it into her face.

...that's fair.

They were quiet for a while, staring blankly out the window while the room around them tilted drunkenly then slowly evened out. After a few minutes Evie got the pitcher of water, and they slowly emptied that as well. When at last things were steady, he shot her a sideways glance.

"You could have told me."

She bit her lip, going out on a limb.

"Technically speaking, I *did* tell you..."

He gave her a hard look.

"Yeah, I could have told you."

They began playing with opposite sides of the pillow between them, fiddling with the fringe and trying to think rationally, while the whiskey made them inconveniently forthcoming and true.

"You could have at least *whispered* it," he muttered petulantly.

"And how would that have helped?" she demanded with the hint of a smile. "Besides giving you time to run away. How would it have helped if I'd whispered it?"

The fae considered for a moment. "...I could have knocked you out."

They shared a tentative smile.

It had been a gamble in coming, but the princess had never been so relieved for having taken a chance. Yes, he was still angry. Furious. But what she'd proposed was bigger than either one of them could imagine. They would face it together, or they couldn't face it at all.

"Do you really think we'll never be happy?"

Those smiles faded as Ellanden leaned his head back against the bed. The bottle was still dangling from his fingers. They drummed occasionally on the sides before he took another drink.

"I think that wretched fishmonger is right," he finally answered. "We broke the hearts of the realm by leaving...it's only fitting that we'd sacrifice our own in return."

Evie glanced at him with a surge of emotion, but could think of nothing to say.

The problem was that it was all a matter of perspective. All a matter of intention. And a great deal of it had been out of their hands. Her spontaneous proposal was a bit of all three.

But to commit oneself to an unwanted marriage was hard enough when done for the right reasons. To dismiss the larger picture as mere penance and do such a thing out of guilt?

Asher was right. He hates himself for leaving. This is punishment, nothing more.

"I wanted to apologize," he continued suddenly, "for leaving the meeting yesterday. I just couldn't..." He trailed off, staring vacantly at a painting on the wall. "Evie...I don't know how I'm going to do it."

His raw honesty laid her bare. It helped a great deal that he'd called her Evie. She moved the pillow and scooted closer, taking his hand with a sigh. He stared down at their entwined fingers.

"I want to have a child with Freya," he whispered. She looked at him with a start and he shook his head slowly, still staring at their hands. "In ten years, twenty years. After a night of heavy drinking, we'd wake up the next morning and realize we both made a tragic mistake."

She laughed quietly, squeezing his hand.

Yes, that's exactly how Ellanden would have a child.

"I want you to have a child with Asher."

Her smile vanished and her skin went cold. "...have you seen him?"

There was a hitch in Ellanden's breathing.

"Once," he answered softly. "He came to my room and asked me not to go through with it."

Evie nodded in silence.

She could only imagine how that meeting went. A vampire appearing on one's windowsill in the dead of night. She would have been surprised if the fae hadn't snatched up a blade.

"He asked you?" she repeated.

The fae grimaced.

Asked was a delicate way of phrasing it. The vampire had instructed, requested, threatened, commanded, begged... There had been no end to what he'd done.

"He's wrong," she said with sudden determination. "Ellanden...it doesn't have to be all or nothing. All four of us know what this is, we all understand why it has to be done."

"But you can't—"

"Listen to me," she insisted. "We'll live together, dine together, travel together, summer together—all the things we do anyway right now. We'll sit on matching thrones, hold up our hands, and the people will have a reason to rally behind us. We'll unite their armies, dispatch my homicidal uncle, destroy that wretched stone...and be *done* with it. All that, for the price of a ring."

He flashed a sad smile, wishing very much that were true.

"I don't think Asher will see it that way. I don't think Freya—"

"You don't need to stop seeing Freya," she said quickly. "And I don't need to stop seeing Asher. This marriage is just a performance. A symbolic gesture to pacify the people. Behind closed doors...we can continue living exactly the way that we were."

He laughed a bit hysterically, burying his face in his hands. "Exactly the way I always imagined my marriage..."

Her heart ached and she rubbed comforting circles on his back. Never had she seen him so defeated. It was as though the very seams of him were falling apart.

"And what of the rest of it?" he asked in a whisper. "When it comes time to have children?"

She froze for a manic second, then shook the bottle.

"We'll get *really* drunk."

He laughed again, but this time the smile lingered a while as he took it from her hands and examined it once again. He was tired. She hadn't realized that before. She wondered if he'd slept.

"Do you remember the first time we went down to those cellars?" he asked suddenly.

She smiled in return, having just visited the memory herself.

"It was just the three of us."

It's always been the three of us.

"Do you think..." he hesitated uncertainly, flashing her a quick look. "Do you think this changes things, with the prophecy?"

Three shall set out, though three shall not return.

"I don't know," she admitted. "But unless we do this, unless we take this step...then it won't matter. Because no one will be standing beside us. And everyone we care about will die."

How's that for a guilt-free perspective?

He took a deep breath, then nodded.

"So we'll...get married."

Strangely enough, it helped to say the words aloud. She braced against them, then pushed abruptly to her feet—reaching down to help him up as well.

"Yes, we will."

Their eyes met for a moment before they shot in opposite directions. Now that the decision had been made it seemed there was an endless list of things to do, plans to make, people to tell...yet they both were standing there, completely frozen.

After what felt like an eternity, she tilted her head to the door.

"Well, I should probably—"

"You've been alone in this," he interrupted abruptly. "Everyone was discussing it, everyone seemed to want it, but somehow...you've been alone."

He crossed the space between them and took her hand. "I won't leave you alone again. You have my word."

Chapter 8

It was the kind of decision that should have happened at the end of a long night, whispered over the light of a dying candle, so that both parties could have retreated with a weary breath and taken solace in a few hours of darkness, surrendering themselves to the embrace of a restless sleep.

But the princess and the fae decided to wed just a short while after sunrise, a depressingly pragmatic omen, soured by the nauseating taste of whiskey drank too soon.

"...this was a mistake," Ellanden murmured, rubbing his eyes.

Evie shot him a quick glance, straightening her dress in the mirror. "Don't say that yet, we're only a few minutes in..." She paused suddenly, gazing at him in the reflection. "Wait—do you mean the marriage? Or the bottle?"

There was an incriminating pause.

"The bottle."

They didn't speak so much after that.

Faint noises could be heard from the rest of the villa. Those who hadn't been awake were rising slowly, while the others had completed their early morning tasks and were summoning the strength for a second wind, speaking in soft voices as they gathered in the kitchen.

"We should tell someone," Ellanden said abruptly, staring at the door as if he could see right through. "We should tell...*everyone*, I suppose."

The princess nodded slowly, fighting a rising wave of dread.

It was one thing to agree to such a thing half-drunk in the privacy of one's chambers. It was quite another to declare it in public, adding the weight of a thousand silent expectations. She was also reluctant to give Melkins the satisfaction of having persuaded them to walk down the aisle.

"I have a good idea," she said suddenly. "What if we told everyone we'd eloped and it was already over? Then we could fulfill the prophecy and tell them we were joking once it was done."

In spite of the panic wreaking havoc on his brain and the alcohol wreaking havoc on his body, the Prince of the Fae managed a little smile.

"You should really stop having ideas. They're not your forte."

She brushed this off with her usual indifference. "That's hardly a way to speak to your future wife."

A sudden hush fell over the room, freezing them both where they stood. For a few terrible seconds, they were unable to see past it. Then they flashed a quick glance from opposite corners.

"...too soon?"

Ellanden didn't answer. He simply finished lacing up his boots before arming himself, rather ostentatiously, with a knife. The princess eyed the blade before clearing her throat casually.

"I have a new servant."

He gave her a blank stare. "...congratulations?"

She flushed in spite of herself. "No, I mean...I was assigned a fae to attend me at the villa. I could send for her, have her send word to all the people we might wish to tell first. Our parents, the Council, a priest—"

"I need to tell Freya."

She froze where she stood, feeling a phantom sting upon her cheek. Her hand drifted absently to touch it, whilst her eyes fixed with heavy resignation the door.

I need to tell Asher.

THEY SPLIT OFF IN SEPARATE directions, agreeing to meet back in an hour's time. A rather insistent part of them wished to drag things out and stall as long as possible; the princess had been only half-joking when she'd seized upon the notion it might be better to simply lie. But it wasn't possible to lie to a fae—let alone an entire kingdom of them—and when dealing with an eternal people it was best to avoid that kind of long-standing grudge. Given all that, and now that the terms had been set, they were anxious for it to be over and done. The days had a way of blending casually together on the lovely island, but the rest of the realm was feeling the sharp urgency of their plight.

If they must be wed, then let it happen quickly. Then the alliance would be settled.

And the prophecy could finally be fulfilled.

"Will you be all right?" Ellanden asked at the last possible second, doubling back to catch her wrist. A strange expression clouded his face. "Do you want me to go with you...to tell him?"

It was a testament to his last encounter with the seething vampire that he wasn't eager for the princess to face him alone. But it wasn't a conversation for three people, it was only for two.

"No, I can do it."

If I can find him.

"But thank you," she added suddenly as he began to walk away. He paused in the hall and their eyes met. "Thank you for all of it, Ellanden. I never..." She trailed off. "I'm really sorry."

He was in front of her the next instant, blowing her hair back with the speed. Despite their recent plunge into chaos, he seemed surprisingly calm. As if the decision itself was the hardest part.

Not all the heartbreak that came next.

"You don't need to thank me," he said softly. "This wasn't your idea, not really, and you're not the one to blame. I told you before and I meant it—we're in this together."

She nodded shakily, echoing a childhood oath. "Till the end?"

He surprised them both with a genuine smile. "Till the bitter end."

On that parting note, the two set off in different directions. He headed not to the witch's chambers but to Cosette's, thinking he might have better luck finding her, while Evie pulled in a deep breath and started off towards Asher's bedroom at the far end of the hall.

The corridor seemed to lengthen the further she went—as if she could have walked forever but never reach the actual end. A part of her didn't see the point. She didn't think she'd actually find him. That magnetic draw of the bond had faded and he didn't want to be found. That's why she was surprised when she pushed open the door to see a vampire standing in the middle of the room.

His hands were folded behind his back and he was staring with fixed attention out the open window, all his senses homing on to something she couldn't see. She paused in the doorway, staring at the back of those dark waves of hair, then slipped inside and cleared her throat.

"...Asher?"

The vampire startled and turned around—revealing not her boyfriend, but his father. She paled in surprise, then flushed almost as quickly. Since the citadel, the two of them had yet to speak.

"I'm sorry," she stammered, "I thought you were..." The name caught in her throat, like it was actually trying to strangle her. "Do you know where he is?"

Aidan regarded her with a truly indecipherable expression. On the outside, he was merely impassive. Only someone who looked closer could see the rage of feeling behind those dark eyes.

"Are you going through with it?" he asked quietly.

She froze a second longer, then nodded.

"Then I doubt very much that he'll return."

Her head bowed as the rest of her crumbled internally. It was suddenly impossible to think of what she might have said to him otherwise. It was impossible to breathe past the whiskey on her lips. There was a painful throb of silence then she nodded again, unable to meet her uncle's eyes.

"I'm sorry—"

"You must not apologize," he interrupted quietly, stepping away from the window. In the fresh light, he looked unimaginably tired. She wondered the last time he'd fed. "But you cannot expect him to stay, either. To watch you and Ellanden marry, start a life together, have children."

He trailed off and she raised her eyes.

"You are bonded with my son, Everly. You cannot expect him to stay for all of that."

Her vision blurred with tears as her heart quickened in panic. She had expected things to be painful, even excruciating. But she'd never dreamt Asher would simply disappear.

Where would he even go? To that hollowed-out mountain? To live with the rest of his kind?

Unable to ask the question, she latched on to the nearest thing.

"But he can't just leave," she said with a touch of hysteria. "The prophecy—"

"He will fulfill the prophecy," Aidan interrupted again, more gently this time. "He has a sense of duty, the same as you. But that will be the end of it."

A harsh note of silence echoed between them. It was not of the vampire's making, but the princess' own labored breathing. For despite the scented breeze, it felt as though there was little air.

He can't just leave. He can't just disappear.

Aidan left the window and swept gracefully past her, pulling open the door. It looked as though he was going to leave without saying anything further, but he paused just outside the frame.

"Evie...that will *have* to be the end of it. Do you understand?"

Their eyes met for an instant.

She nodded in reply.

"In that case, you'd better go to the courtyard," he said quietly, eyes drifting past her towards the open sky. "There are people here to speak with you."

THE TABLE WAS SET JUST the way it had been a day before—with Leonor and Cassiel on one side, Melkins on the other, and Dylan pacing like an angry lion in between.

He was still smarting about the reprimand. No doubt the note was in his pocket.

They had come without being summoned. Never a good sign, but in this case their work was already done. In those painful early hours, the friends had already put the matter to bed.

...so to speak.

The princess froze where she was standing, lingering in the hall just out of sight. For one of the first times, she saw past the immediate logistics and wondered fearfully as to what came next.

Like a distant warning, Ellanden's voice echoed in her mind.

And what of the rest of it? When it comes time to have children?

Ironically enough, it might have been easier to handle just a few weeks earlier, before she'd had any experience with such matters. Before she and Asher had shared a bed. Then it would have been a nameless fear—vague and hypothetical. Now she had too many details at her disposal, too much personal knowledge as to the progression towards such intimacy. The things she might expect.

...with Ellanden.

She could not imagine attempting such a thing with her childhood friend. Under any circumstances. Plied with any amount of whiskey. She could not imagine the two of them—

"Evie?"

She jumped a mile, then looked up to see the collection of men staring at her curiously from the courtyard. It was her father who had called her name, his face tightening with a look of concern.

"We were just about to send for you," he continued, taking a step forward. "Is this—"

"We were about to send for you ourselves," she blurted awkwardly. "The two of us. Ellanden and I. We were talking this morning, and...why don't I go find him?"

If the men were curious before, those breathless, stilted sentences had left them downright alarmed. Cassiel and Leonor exchanged a quick look, while Melkins continued examining her as if something might have broken in her head. Her father nodded slowly, trying to follow along.

"All right," he said softly, stepping towards the hall. "I can come with you—"

"No, that's okay," she cut him off quickly, backing away at the same time. "I'll only be a moment. Then we can...we can sort all this out."

She scampered back up the hall without a backwards glance, leaving them staring in silence behind her. Not until she was safely on the other side of the sprawling villa did she finally pause to take a breath. Both hands curled into sudden fists, pressing against the lids of her eyes.

Why did I think we could do this?!

A silent scream welled up inside her but she forced it back down, stilling to sudden attention as the sound of hushed voices drifted into the hall. One was soft and pleading, while the other was clipped and burnt. She ghosted towards the room in question, staring through the crack in the door.

"—doesn't have to be that way," Ellanden was saying, desperately holding on to Freya's clenched hands. "You know how I feel for Everly, you know there isn't that kind of love between us. This is an alliance, Frey. Nothing more. It doesn't—"

"This is a *marriage*, Ellanden." She yanked her hands free, glaring up in cold fury. "If that hasn't been made clear to you, then perhaps you should talk again to your beloved council."

Evie shrank back as he bowed his head, ivory hair spilling into his eyes.

"I can't let it happen," he said softly. "I can't let them die. If they won't fight beside each other without such a declaration, then the dragon wins. There isn't another—"

"So you've said," she interrupted shortly. "Why are you still here?"

He looked up blankly, like he was out of breath.

"What do you—"

"Why aren't you with your *fiancée*?" she hissed. "If there isn't another way, if the decision's already been made, then what are you still doing here with me?"

He flinched like she'd slapped him. "I...I needed to tell you."

She nodded sharply. "You've told me."

A tremble shook through the fae's body, visible even from the door. His breath caught in his chest, and though the princess couldn't see it his face must have been a sight to behold.

"This doesn't have to be an end," he said quietly, staring at the floor. "I...I love you, Freya. I don't know how to—" He caught himself quickly, trying to even his voice to speak. "We could live in separate kingdoms, she and I. You would never have to—"

The witch held up her hand, taking a measured breath. "You burst into my life, only to vanish for ten years. At last I find you again, but you refuse to look at me because I'm mortal. You finally come to see reason—coming into my heart, coming into my bed—only to promise yourself for all eternity to another."

She shook her head slowly, eyes blurring with tears.

"I am finished with you, Ellanden."

Before he could say a word in response she was gone, leaving him standing right where she left him in the center of the room. His hands were shaking, but the rest of him was perfectly still. An unnatural kind of stillness. As if he was no longer breathing. As if a part of him had simply died.

The sound of voices echoed from the courtyard and Evie bowed her head.

How can this be the way?

"...Ellanden?"

He startled, but didn't turn.

"I'm so sorry," she called softly, "but they're waiting for us outside."

There was a beat of silence.

"Just give me a moment."

She slid noiselessly into the hallway, waiting as he stared with fixed determination at the ceiling, gathering himself and wiping his eyes. When he appeared a moment later his entire face had changed in a way she didn't understand, in a way she didn't think was possible.

"Let's go."

She jumped a little and stared up at him, unable to keep pace. The fae looked better suited to lie down and rest for the next few years, but his eyes were hard and he was already moving.

"Let's *go*, Everly. I want to get this over with."

THERE WAS PROBABLY a procedure to such a declaration, but the children didn't know it and they were short on time. The moment they set foot in the courtyard, Ellanden glanced around the table and simply announced the thing himself.

"Everly and I have decided to get married."

Everly again. Evie was gone.

Or so she thought.

In an act that surprised them both, he reached down suddenly and took her hand—keeping his eyes fixed on the men standing around the table. Mclkins looked as smugly pleased as they had both anticipated, but the rest of them were nothing short of astonished.

"You have?" Cassiel repeated, unable to keep from phrasing it as a question. Unbeknownst to the others, he'd been awake half the night discussing the matter with his wife, trying to find a way to undo it. "I had expected us to consider things further—"

"There's no time," Ellanden said shortly. "This is about the prophecy, and we are already ten years behind schedule. If I'd known such madness would be required, Evie and I would have eloped somewhere on the road—gotten it all behind us."

Something he was clearly eager to do now.

"And you?" Dylan asked softly, eyes never leaving his daughter. "You have agreed to this?"

She took a deep breath, clinging to the fae's fingers.

"I suggested it, didn't I?" She tried to keep her voice light, even making a passable attempt at a smile. "Ellanden's right, we haven't any more time to linger. Let's finish this and be done."

Considering they'd been prepared to helm the meeting, steering the younger generation through it as best they could, the adults were at a bit of a loss. *Some* of them. The matchmaker was still staring between them with a brittle smile, but it was Leonor who pushed to his feet.

"We can make the announcement at the citadel this evening." His eyes flew apologetically between them. "Such a thing was expected, so the preparations have already been made."

Of course they have.

"Good," Ellanden said briskly. His voice was even, but his hand shook in hers. "Is there anything further? Or may we be excused?"

He might have wanted to depart before the others could smell the alcohol on his breath. Or perhaps he merely wanted to bury his face in a pillow and scream.

Whatever the reason, the princess was on exactly the same page.

"Yes, are we finished?" she echoed, unable to meet her father's eyes. "There are several things I wish to attend to before—"

"Of course, my dear," Melkins interrupted, pushing slowly to his feet. "There are just a few small matters left to discuss. Mainly, your living arrangements until the wedding."

...what?

She and Ellanden had already been angling towards the door. But they froze dead still at his words, shooting each other a swift look before turning instinctively to their parents.

"Our living arrangements?" she repeated uncertainly. "Could we not just stay as we are? I mean, our entire family is housed in this place together—"

Melkins chuckled as if she'd made a joke, shaking his head with amusement.

"No, child. The bride and groom may not sleep under the same roof until they have been properly joined before the eyes of the people. Such a thing would be wildly inappropriate."

...are you serious?

Evie stared back at him in stunned silence.

She didn't know which was worse, his casual use of such volatile words or his demand that one of them be summarily evicted, lest there should be even the slightest hint of impropriety.

We'll soon be required to take off each other's clothes, but heaven forbid we sleep atop the same mountain.

"Inappropriate?" Ellanden echoed dangerously. He had released her hand and it looked very much like he wanted to strangle the man on the spot. "*That's* what you think is—"

"There's also the matter of a dowry."

Cassiel and Dylan exchanged a quick look. As many times as they'd teased each other about such a prospect over the years, such a word had never been uttered between them.

"Customarily," Melkins continued obliviously, "a fitting tribute would have been sent from Belaria. Naturally, no such arrangements have been made. But there is still time—"

At that point, Leonor thought it wise to intervene.

"The children have shared a nursery, and for the last ten years they've been travelling together across the realm. I think we can trust there will be no indecency between them. And as for the other matter, the Kingdom of the Fae would be happy to excuse such a gift."

He shot a confirmatory glance at Cassiel, who nodded curtly.

"Then I believe our business is finished." The councilman pushed to his feet, effectively ending the meeting. "We can reconvene at sundown to make the formal announcement. That is all."

A look of scandal flitted across Melkins' face, but before he could open his mouth to argue Leonor repeated the words in a voice that left no question.

"That is all."

Ellanden barely waited for him to finish speaking before he turned around and swept quickly from the courtyard. It was so sudden the princess might have thought he was furious with her once again, if he hadn't given her hand a final squeeze before he left. She stared after him a few seconds before shooting her father a parting look and followed right after him—keeping her pace even and her face steady until she was safely behind the closed door of her room.

At that point, she slumped to the floor and sobbed.

Chapter 9

The city of Taviel was ablaze with excitement, but the princess never saw it. She stayed on the balcony of her chambers, watching the sun drift slowly across the sky.

There had been many attempts to speak with her.

Both parents had come together, but stayed only long enough to see their daughter would rather be left alone. Adelaide had tried her luck next, bringing with her a small luncheon before eventually leaving as well. The ones who'd gotten the farthest were actually Seth and Cosette, but neither of them had any idea what to say, and they left her just as distraught as when they'd arrived.

When at last the sky began to darken, there was a quiet knock on the door.

"I'm not trying to be dramatic, I promise," Evie called with a little sigh. "I'd honestly just rather have some time by myself."

There was a pause, then the door opened and Leia slipped inside.

"I understand that, milady." The fae bowed her head apologetically. "Only, the day's sun has nearly set and I've come to help you prepare."

Already?

The princess cast a frightened look out the window, only to see she was right.

The sun had slipped almost completely behind the horizon and tiny dots of torchlight were springing up all over the city, as though some kind of evening flower was coming into bloom.

"Do you know how it's supposed to happen?" she asked nervously, watching as the fae breezed back and forth across the room. "Must I...make a speech or something?"

Leia shook her head reassuringly. "Not at all, Your Highness. I'm assuming no one walked you through it, because your own participation is rather minimal. You will stand beside the prince as our head of council announces the betrothal. You'll wave and smile, then you can retire for the night in peace."

Your own participation is rather minimal.

Evie clenched her jaw with a wry smile. "There's irony for you…"

The fae glanced up from the bureau. "Pardon?"

She shook her head. "Nothing, just talking to myself."

The next half hour was spent in virtual silence.

The princess allowed herself to be moved like a puppet, staring vacantly into space as Leia gently and efficiently took her through the paces—scrubbing away the tears and whiskey, and giving her a polished shine. Halfway through, the fae insisted that she eat something. When that was finally finished, she made her drink something as well—coaxing tiny sips of a calming, herbal tea.

Evie gripped the cup reassuringly and allowed her mind to wander, listening to the distant sounds of the city, wondering if Ellanden was receiving the same soothing treatment as well.

There was one person she didn't consider, one name she didn't allow herself to think. After speaking that morning with Aidan, she wasn't sure if her boyfriend was still anywhere in the city.

For that matter…she wasn't sure if he was still her boyfriend.

He can't be. You can't have a boyfriend and a fiancé at the same time.

"There," Leia murmured, stepping back to admire her work, "that should do it." She tilted her head to consider before turning to the vanity. "Perhaps a circlet for your hair…"

Evie blinked back to the present, watching as the fae searched the drawers. They weren't standing anywhere close to the mirror, but regardless of whatever had been done there wasn't a chance in the world she could look half as lovely as the person charged with dressing her.

How foolish I must look, she thought distractedly, *standing beside someone like Ellanden. How foolish I will look to all his people…a mortal girl set to wear an immortal crown.*

To be honest, it was more of a resigned observation than a note of actual despair. Her problems had increased in pitch, to the point where she was no longer worried about the cosmetic.

After all...would I not have looked just as foolish with someone like Asher?

With a wistful smile, she reached out a secret finger to touch a lock of the fae's silken hair.

"Milady?"

Leia turned immediately, looking at the princess in surprise.

"Sorry." She blushed, lowering her eyes like a wayward child. "I wasn't thinking."

The fae regarded her another moment before lifting a strand of diamonds. They were leaves, Evie realized, twisting gracefully together like a tendril of the most delicate vine.

"Might I make a suggestion, Your Highness?" the fae asked lightly, placing the shimmering gems atop her head. "Focus not on the wedding itself...but on what comes after."

Evie shot her a look of alarm, and the fae shook her head quickly.

"I don't mean *immediately* after," she clarified. "I meant...the reason you left all those years ago. The reason you've returned. Focus on the prophecy."

Dragons and hellfire, darkness and destruction...?

The fae was right, it actually calmed her down.

"It's the reason for all of this," Evie murmured, feeling a bit steadier. "The single thing that's been driving us all this time. But now that we're finally home, it's like no one's even thinking of it."

Leia laughed quietly, adjusting the glittering stones.

"No one's *speaking* of it," she corrected, "not here in the villa. But much is being done in the rest of the city. They started preparing things before you'd even arrived."

Evie looked at her curiously.

"Like what?" she asked a bit bashfully. "You're right…no one speaks of it to me."

"After ten years, I suppose they wanted to give you children a break." The fae rifled in the closet before emerging with a pair of shoes. "Food is being stockpiled, supplies are relocated, the villagers in more remote regions have gathered closer to the cities. Most of the preparations involve the army, but those who serve in other ways throughout the kingdom have fortified as well."

Evie held on to her shoulder for balance, stepping into the shoes.

"I saw a group of officers taking stock of equipment in the armory," she volunteered, feeling energized for the first time in days. "I'm assuming my parents' kingdoms are doing the same."

The woman nodded thoughtfully.

"My people were preparing to fight this enemy alone. Ever since news of Lord Cassiel's return the troops have been readying for departure, mobilizing units, saying goodbyes…"

Their eyes met in the sudden quiet.

"My people have a saying," the fae continued softly. "'There is a time for peace and a time for war, but there is never long in between'. Many centuries have I roamed this earth, Your Highness, but seldom have I known such heartbreak as the last few years. When the Carpathians attacked, we took up our swords. When the giants came, we took up our bows. When news arrived of this latest threat, we prepared to fight yet again…but there seemed little hope in it. You are changing that tonight."

They stared a moment longer, then the fae offered up a gentle smile.

"Think on that, when you are standing in the citadel."

The last of the preparations were finished in silence, just a touch here and there. A flutter of nerves began stirring in Evie's stomach, but despite what lay ahead of her she was oddly calm.

"We?" she asked suddenly. Leia looked up with a question. "You said...*we* prepared to fight yet again. Did you fight in the army? Are you coming with us to the Dunes?"

Centuries the woman has been alive. She couldn't have gone all that time without lifting a blade.

The fae pushed back to her feet, eyes shining in the dusky light. "My people have another saying: *'felia tarsec ne rowe, mia sankering te votev niressa'.*"

The princess smiled, this one she knew.

"Every fae is a warrior," she answered. "They just busy themselves in between."

Leia nodded her head, then turned the princess towards the mirror. "And now, Your Highness...you are ready."

EVIE HURRIED DOWN THE steps of the villa towards the ivory citadel, lifting the skirts of her gown as her feet flew over the polished stone. The rest of her family had already been seated but she was to enter last with Ellanden, so the High Council could introduce them as they arrived.

Just a few quick words, then on to the business of saving the realm.

That was the phrase everyone kept telling her. By the time she started rushing towards the gleaming tower, she found herself chanting it under her breath.

A lone voice was already speaking inside the citadel, a rather solemn speech by the sound of it, though she couldn't make out much that was said. She circled around to the back entrance as she had been instructed, then abruptly panicked until she saw the back of Ellanden's hair.

"Thank the heavens," she gasped, racing up behind him, "and spare me your lecture on punctuality. *You* should try running in these shoes—"

He turned around to greet her, then stepped back in surprise.

"What have you...? No lecture." His dark eyes swept over her, softening with an expression she'd rarely seen. "You look lovely."

Her immortal attendant had apparently read more into that discarded dress selection than the princess had realized at the time, because the gown she'd commissioned was a stunning blend of their two worlds. A glimmering cascade of leaf-green silk that hung loose off her shoulders and was draped low to expose the length of her back. The sleeves were nothing more than shimmer, sliced up the middle to fall freely down both sides of her arms. And while the neck was a high, straight line across her shoulder blades, her fiery hair had been spun into delicate waves to frame each side.

The circlet had been the final exquisite touch—curving gently around her forehead as if some master with a spare bit of starlight had painted the skin with a stroke of his brush.

She was both princess and queen. Both mortal and eternal. A bridge between two worlds.

Wherever that may lead.

Ellanden hesitated uncertainly a moment, then pressed a kiss to her cheek.

"Careful," she teased, but she held on to his shirt, feeling suddenly unsteady. "We wouldn't want to do anything inappropriate."

The voice swelled in volume behind them, followed by a round of applause.

"It's strange," he murmured, keeping their heads close. "I should be happy right now. A man I've known my entire life is about to announce my engagement to a girl I love. My heart is broken, and I don't know if it will ever be the same...but seeing you now, a part of me *is* happy."

He stared inquisitively into her eyes.

"Happy we are together, I suppose. Is that frightfully selfish?"

She squeezed his hands. "You are a frightfully selfish person."

He laughed softly, then they turned their heads at the same time. The speech had concluded and Leonor had stepped onto the podium, and they heard the gentle cadence of his voice.

"This is it," she murmured, smoothing down her dress. "No turning back now." She tilted her head towards the woods with the hint of a grin. "You want to make a run for it?"

He laughed again, pulling in a steadying breath. "Why do you still ask questions like that, when you can turn into a dragon?"

That's a good point.

The councilman's voice rang out over the crowd and they took a step closer together, staring through a small window in the door. The citadel was packed to the brim, nothing but an endless sea of smiling faces—as if the entire city had somehow crammed itself inside.

A shiver ran up Evie's spine as her own words echoed back to her—quickening her pulse as they struck her anew. This truly was the point of no return. In a few brief moments she and the fae would be officially engaged, soon to be married...with the weight of an empire resting upon it.

"I feel like I'm going to pass out," she breathed, tapping her fingertips nervously against the shimmering folds of her gown. "Think you can just carry me?"

He flashed a sudden, boyish grin. "When have I ever *not* carried you?"

For whatever reason, it turned out to be the perfect thing to say. Her breathing slowed, the world stopped spinning, and the two of them shared a final, suspended look.

Then they took each other's hands and walked onto the stage.

It was *pandemonium*.

The second they appeared, the crowd leapt to their feet—cheering at such a deafening volume it drowned out the sound of the falls. Each ringing shout echoed off the ivory stone, amplifying and bouncing back, until the noise could be heard from every corner of the island.

Somewhere deep in the woods, a lonely vampire lifted his head.

"Peace, my friends."

It couldn't have been possible to hear Leonor over the commotion, but the second he opened his mouth to speak a sudden hush fell over the chamber. His eyes swept over them, more relieved than he'd ever admit that they'd both actually arrived, before brightening with a rare smile.

"Time is of the essence, so I'll keep my remarks brief."

He bowed low to his prince, beckoning with strict formality towards the princess.

"Ellanden Elénarin, Crown Prince of the Fae and heir to the Kreo throne, allow me to present Everly Hale-Damaris, High Princess of—"

"There is no need to introduce us," Ellanden interrupted quietly. His dark eyes fastened upon hers, twinkling with a little smile. "She's my best friend."

A slight deviation from the script, but the people seemed to appreciate the candor. At any rate, it was the first time the princess managed a genuine smile in return.

"You did this last time," he continued softly, each word whispering over the stones to reach even those in the back of the room. "But I believe the honor traditionally belongs to me."

There was a quiet burst of laughter, a sea of glowing smiles from every single person in the citadel...except those standing in the front row. The front row was reserved for family.

There were no smiles there.

"Everly," he caught himself abruptly, the last of the sunset catching in his eyes, "*Evie*."

Her breath caught as he sank onto one knee.

"Would you marry me?"

GRIEVANCE

THE CITY OF TAVIEL didn't rest that night. Every man, woman, and child in the ivory capital took to the streets in celebration, the likes of which carried on until the early traces of dawn.

The princess stayed as long as she was required before slipping into the woods, wandering along the forest trail, until at last the final echoes faded into an otherwise peaceful night.

I can't believe that just happened. I can't believe it's actually done.

She went along the winding path without having any real idea where she was going, drifting between patches of silvery trees as a secret world came to life beneath the light of the moon.

Alders lowered their arms and stood straight as arrows, clusters of blackthorn and long trails of willow hung in suspension, bathing the woods around them in a reflective glow. The river itself was nothing more than a ribbon, looping occasionally round the base of the path as it whispered and tumbled over ancient stone, making its endless journey to the waves of the distant sea.

Evie lifted her eyes as a silver-tipped wren took to the skies above her, keeping well away from the other creatures of the forest that awoke to hunt at night. Sweet-scented civets with quills of poison. Blue-tongued foxes that changed color depending on whether they were in shadow or light.

Taviel had a way of blending realities that as an imperious princess of the High Kingdom, a meat-eating wolf of Belaria, she could hardly approve. It illuminated the darkness, breathing life into metaphor in a way that made things far too poetic and literal for her taste.

I must get used to such things. If I'm to wear their crown.

She kept the wren in sight as long as she was able before lowering her gaze to see someone else watching as well. She hadn't realized how far she'd wandered, or where her feet had taken her.

But that was the way of the whispering well…one never arrived there by mistake.

"Asher."

The vampire was sitting in the trees not far from the ancient stone, staring down into the glassy waters. In daylight, he burned with contrasts—shockingly fair skin, and hair so dark it seemed to steal all the light around it—but in the moon, he was all silver.

"I heard the cheering," he replied without lifting his eyes. "Did you say yes?"

She took a seat beside him, settling lightly among the ferns. For a long time, it was quiet between them. Then he flashed her a sideways look, his lips hardening into a wry smile.

"There's my answer," he said softly. "You look like a fae princess."

She stared down at her dress, suddenly wishing she'd changed into something else before ghosting into woods. Her fingers twisted together as she tried to think of anything to say in return, but the vampire didn't seem to require her to say anything. He merely leaned back on his hands, stretching his long legs in front of him as those dark eyes drifted once again to the trees.

"Such a shame this should happen here," he said suddenly, looking oddly detached from the actual feeling of such a thing. "This was always my favorite place. I always wanted to come here."

She stared at him in silence, eyes dilating in the dark.

"I thought the High Kingdom was your favorite," she finally managed. "You told me that you always wanted to come—"

"I always wanted to see you."

But he doesn't now.

They sat for a while longer, settling into those far-flung shadows as people occasionally made their way past on the trail. The well was far outside the walls of the city, but its waters were never vacant for long. For centuries, people had travelled through the realm to gaze into its reflective surface. Seeking answers to questions and speaking to loved ones whose time had passed by.

After what felt like a very long time, Asher spoke to her again.

"What are you doing here?"

"Wandering," she answered. "What are you doing here?"

"Watching."

He gestured to the trail and she looked on in silence as an older woman knelt in the soft grass beside the water, weeping quietly into her hands. The minutes dragged past as she rocked back and forth, then someone younger melted out of the trees and gently led her away.

"Did you make a wish?" the princess asked before she could stop herself.

Since they were children, they'd been whispering secrets into that well. Demanding blessings from a higher power, walking away with chins lifted, as if they'd gained some greater understanding of themselves. It was mostly posturing, but there had been some pensive moments as well.

Ellanden had gone there after his governess died. Her mother had gone after Abel Bishop.

Instead of answering, the vampire pushed soundlessly to his feet—pacing further into the trees. The princess bolted up after him, but froze on the edge of the forest trail.

"Your father says you're leaving," she called to the back of his head. "He says that once the prophecy is fulfilled...you could never be expected to stay."

Asher paused mid-step, staring into the trees. "Can you blame me?"

She let out a breath as her eyes spilled over with tears. "...where would you go?"

His body tensed like a burn but he kept his gaze on that moonlit forest, wishing with all his heart that he wasn't trapped on a lovely island as the girl he loved prepare to marry another. Wishing that he couldn't feel *her* heart breaking as a kingdom of immortals celebrated on the streets.

For a split second, he almost turned to face her. Then he stalked into the darkening trees.

"Don't bother with the well," he called over his shoulder. "The thing's broken."

Chapter 10

Evie made it back to the villa just a little after dawn, and it seemed she'd no sooner closed her eyes than she was gently being shaken awake again.

"Not today," she mumbled, smashing a pillow over her face without even bothering to open her eyes. "Today, I stay in this bed and dream of death."

There was a pause, then a hand shook her again.

The pillow was pitifully surrendered and she squinted upwards to see the smiling face of her mother. Well, it wasn't *smiling* exactly. But the woman was clearly amused.

"Dream of death?" she repeated lightly.

Evie bit her lip and glanced at the bedspread. "...it's a figure of speech."

A tray of food was already waiting at the foot of the bed. No doubt the queen had been prowling the corridors early and intercepted her attendant, choosing to deliver breakfast herself.

She hoisted herself higher, staring down in dismay. "Did you take my peaches?"

"Get up," Katerina replied, offering a hand at the same time. When it was refused, she used it instead to rip away the covers. "Get *up*, Evie. We have a busy day planned."

The princess countered with an icy glare and anchored herself to the bed.

Her mother had been the only person at the celebration yesterday who hadn't made an effort to pretend as though things were fine. She had stayed glued to her daughter's arm for the entire duration, and was the one who'd helped her escape into the forest when the time was right.

She'd thought they were on the same page. She'd thought her mother had understood.

But she's clearly a monster.

"A busy day?" she repeated dispiritedly, sitting up and rubbing her eyes. "I wasn't joking, Mom, I can't...I can't have another *busy* day, all right? I need some time to myself."

...and some peaches.

Katerina paused beside the bed, gazing down with a tortured expression her distractible daughter would never see. By the time the princess had given up on her stolen breakfast and turned back around, her face had cleared with a deceptively bright smile.

"If you're saying that you wouldn't like to stand on another podium and vow to marry your childhood playmate, I don't blame you. But that's not the kind of *busy* I had in mind..."

A WAR ROOM.

When her mother had first said the fateful words, Evie couldn't believe they were actually true. How many times had she and her friends tried to infiltrate such a place? How many times had they been discovered boosting each other into windows or cramming themselves into the bottom of a food cart, only to be summarily dismissed? Now they were to enter by open invitation?

To participate in the discussion, Katerina had told her. *To take an active role.*

Of course, her disbelieving daughter had made her repeat this several times—swearing on each occasion that she was actually telling the truth. Unfortunately, by the time they'd finally reached some kind of understanding, Katerina was conscripted into conversation with a trio of warlocks and Evie had to walk the rest of the way to the coveted meeting by herself.

Wait...warlocks?

The princess paused in the middle of the pavilion, staring around in shock.

At first glance, it was hardly noticeable. The market was crowded as ever, packed to the brim with an ever-changing rotation of fae. Enchanting men strode purposely across the street, their long cloaks whispering behind them. Ethereal women carrying tiny, cherubic children made their way in and out of stores. Everything was exactly as it had always been in the Ivory City.

But upon a closer look, there were some unexpected guests.

Evie stared in amazement as a coven of witches breezed out of the local bakery, speaking to each other behind sticky fingers as they tore off pieces of honeyed bread. The shifters were almost impossible to miss. Although there were only a few, her father's people always had a slightly rougher shine. One of them was running an incredulous hand over an ivory banister, while another let out such a loud bark of laughter it earned him several looks of disapproval from a group of passing fae.

She was so engrossed in the bizarre scene, she almost didn't notice a shifty-looking goblin slip one of the diamond bracelets she'd been admiring earlier into his satchel.

The two of them locked eyes, then he hurried on his way.

...citizen's arrest?

"Admiring the view?"

She turned in surprise as her grandmother walked towards her with a smile.

Despite the colorful influx of people, there was still something inherently distinctive about Adelaide Grey. She sliced through the crowd with a regal bearing she'd never quite lost during those years in the woods. Never noticing the people who moved deferentially aside to let her pass, never noticing when they turned around to watch her afterwards, whispering under their breath.

"I was just surprised," Evie admitted, glancing back to see that the thieving goblin had disappeared. "I've come to this city almost every year of my life and I can count on one hand the number of people I've met who weren't fae. Did Gran open another portal?"

It took Adelaide a moment to understand who she was referring to. "You mean...the old Kreo priestess?"

Evie nodded distractedly.

"She has about fifty hyphenated names. Gran was always easier to remember."

The hint of a smile drifted across the queen's face.

"She opened one this morning to allow the remaining kingdoms to send representatives to the war council. Most of the organizing will be done on the mainland, but now that the realm has been formally aligned...your father thought it was best if such things were discussed together."

My people were preparing to fight this enemy alone...you are changing that tonight.

The princess glanced instinctively towards the citadel.

"This war council," she began tentatively, "are you going as well?"

Adelaide shook her head with a quick smile.

"There's no longer a reason for me to attend such gatherings; my time in that world has come and passed. I was merely out for an early walk in the forest—"

"That's ridiculous," Evie interrupted in alarm. "You reigned as Queen of the High Kingdom before some of these people were even alive. There is *every* reason for you to be there."

"My darling—"

"There is *every* reason," she repeated firmly, linking their arms together and continuing towards the citadel. "Of course, you might be nervous. I'll need to come along for moral support."

Adelaide's eyes danced with a twinkling smile. "Oh, I see...*I* might be nervous?"

"There is no shame in it," the princess snapped defensively. "You've been out of the game a long time. Who knows what things might have…"

She trailed off, staring towards the trees.

Looks like I'm not the only one spending time with my grandmother.

Two people were standing by themselves beneath a group of flowering chestnuts. The contrast between them couldn't have been greater—a handsome young warrior, caught in the blaze of eternal youth; and a withered old priestess, lined with the wrinkles of a woman who'd spent the last few centuries in a constant smile—yet there was blood between them. They were family.

"Gran," Adelaide murmured, watching with a smile, "…it fits."

The princess took a step closer, surprised to hear they were speaking Fae. Rather, Ellanden was recounting some story, talking a lot with his hands, while his great-grandmother was listening with an uncharacteristically solemn expression, pausing every so often to wipe at her eyes.

A single name jumped out from the rest.

Rone.

Her own grasp of the language was far from fluent. With that perfect vampiric recall, Asher was the one who'd always spoke it best. But the story the prince was sharing became suddenly clear.

He's telling her what happened to the camp on the edge of the sea.

"I was very proud of you yesterday," Adelaide said quietly, following her granddaughter's gaze to the captivating fae. "Although I can't say that I'm particularly pleased. If I've learned a single thing in my life, it's that no good can come from an unwanted marriage."

Evie turned to her in surprise, unsure what to say in return.

"It's not the same as yours," she finally managed, treading lightly upon strange and delicate ground. "I've known Ellanden all my life. He's a good man."

"Yes, but is he the *right* man?" Adelaide answered gently. "Marriage to an immortal is a very long commitment, my dear. You have a single chance to get it right."

The princess flashed her another look before turning back to the trees.

The story had apparently reached its conclusion, because Ellanden gave his grandmother a quick kiss on the cheek and then the two headed off in separate directions. The old priestess made her way towards the citadel, while the fae started walking back up the pavilion steps.

"Think on what I said," Adelaide said softly as he spotted them in the distance and started jogging over. "It's never too late to set things right."

Evie stiffened beside her.

"No offense...but it's *absolutely* too late," she countered. "You were there yesterday, they already made the announcement. And even if they hadn't..." She trailed off hopelessly. "You speak as though it was my decision to make, but it wasn't. This is what the people required of us, this is what we owe them. They wouldn't enter back into an alliance unless this demand was met."

The queen studied her a moment, then offered a parting smile. "That may be true...but it doesn't make it right."

She left without another word, waving in farewell just as Ellanden reached them—striding back across the pavilion towards the bakery the witches had just left.

Supremely unhelpful.

"Good morning," Ellanden said brightly. "Having a good talk with your grandmother?"

Evie stared after the queen with a scowl. "No," she snapped. "You?"

He glanced down at her in surprise. "Uh...no, actually. I was telling her about Rone."

The princess forgot her own troubles immediately, staring at him in concern.

"I heard," she admitted, not wanting to press. "Gran speaks Fae?"

He nodded distractedly, squinting towards the sunrise as the bells in the ivory tower began to clang. "She speaks all kinds of things. Are you going to the war room?"

"War *council*," she corrected importantly. "And yes, I'm apparently indispensable. Are you?"

His face lit up with a trace of its old excitement. "I certainly am. Don't even need to wear a disguise."

She snorted with laughter.

Their childhood attempts to sneak into the meetings covered a wide spectrum, but perhaps the most memorable had been the time when the fae had posed as a linguistically-challenged goblin.

"That doesn't mean you shouldn't."

He laughed as well, but it faded quickly as the gate to that led to the villa opened and a lovely young witch stepped onto the street. She was flanked on both sides by Seth and Cosette, who almost appeared to be guarding her, and though he took an involuntary step towards her he reconsidered almost immediately and headed off towards the citadel instead.

"I'll see you there," he called over his shoulder.

Evie nodded mutely, torn as to which way to go.

The last thing she wanted was another slap across the face, but their little fellowship was trapped on the same island and couldn't avoid each other forever. She had just decided to attempt that first fledging step towards reconciliation, when the path in front of her was suddenly blocked.

"Good morning, Your Highness. And welcome back."

She sucked in a quick breath, freezing on the spot.

Of all the men and women residing in her mother's kingdom, there were only a few who'd ever actually scared her. The mistress who taught embroidery. The pair of twin boys who delivered fresh produce from the countryside and swore they could read each other's minds.

And Miranda Cartwright—a ranking member on the queen's council.

"Good morning," she stammered, still trying to catch her breath. "I wasn't expecting to see you here. My grandmother told me that only—"

"—only the heads of state had been offered a seat at the war council," the woman replied with her usual brisk efficiency. "That is true."

The princess stared at her another moment before it suddenly clicked.

"You replaced Abel Bishop. You became the head of my mother's council."

A look of surprise flitted across the woman's face before settling into a curious expression.

"Ten years ago," she replied. "But of course...you wouldn't have known."

Evie shook her head, suddenly wishing she'd gone with Ellanden after all.

It wasn't that the woman was unkind, she was simply robotic—an unflinching pillar of pragmatism that often left the high-spirited young princess scrambling for her lines.

"No I...I didn't know." She dropped her gaze, struggling to collect herself.

On some level, she'd yet to even process Bishop's death. It had blended so seamlessly into the attack on the caravan and the rest of the prophetic aftermath that there were moments she'd forgotten he'd even died. A man she'd known since birth. To have him replaced with *this* woman?

"Is this your first time in Taviel?" she asked politely, unable to imagine her existing past the palace walls. "There should be some time to—"

"There you are." Cosette appeared from nowhere, sliding her arm into the princess' and offering the councilwoman a polite smile. "I hate to interrupt, but the meeting's about to start."

Only the woodland princess could have disrupted such an exchange, and have both parties leave thinking she was even sweeter than when they'd first arrived. Even the unyielding Miranda Cartwright returned the girl's angelic smile before glancing towards the citadel.

"In that case, I'd better take my leave. But it truly was a blessing to see you again, Your Highness." Her eyes reflected the ivory gleam. "I hear we are to expect great things…"

The two princess watched her depart before turning to each other.

"I forgot to tell you," Cosette muttered. "*She's* in charge now."

"Why her?" Evie demanded. "Why not Rollins?"

The lovely fae lifted her shoulder in a shrug.

"Rollins is a brilliant statesman, but our alliances were crumbling and the realm was on the brink of war," Cosette explained. "They wanted someone with—"

"—with a bit more of a militant flavor," Evie finished grimly, staring at the woman's back with a trace of dislike. "Well, they certainly got that."

Seth and Freya joined them a moment later. At first it looked as though the witch had come of her own choosing. It took a second to realize he was gripping her arm.

"Who was that?" he asked, following their gaze.

"The bane of my existence," Evie muttered.

"The head of the High Kingdom's council," Cosette corrected with the hint of a grin.

Freya stared blankly ahead, as if the rest of the pavilion was empty, while Seth watched the woman a second longer before glancing back at Evie with a twinkling smile.

"You don't like her?"

She let out a martyred sigh, while Cosette elbowed her in the ribs.

"Miranda is one of the few people at court without any tolerance for mischief. Evie was once punished for stealing a bucket of crabs from the kitchens and stuffing them into her shoes."

"I didn't steal them," the princess replied stiffly. "I relocated them. It was metaphorical, not malicious. And you'd think they were still moving from the way she screamed..."

Seth chuckled under his breath while she turned hesitantly to Freya, planning her next words carefully and keeping a casual distance from the girl's hands.

"I'm really glad you came," she began nervously. "I was hoping that—"

"I think I'll find a seat inside," Freya interrupted shortly, speaking only to the other two. She swept through the bunch, then glanced at Evie with an icy smile. "Maybe by your friend Miranda."

IF THE PRINCESS WAS expecting a degree of exclusivity to her first war council, she was sadly mistaken. While the invitation had been extended to all 'heads of state and clan', each of the kingdoms had given that a rather broad interpretation.

The Kreo delegation consisted of faction-leaders: a coven of witches, a power of warlocks, a trio of goblins, and a trinket of dwarves. The Fae were already vastly over-represented, yet insisted most the officers currently residing in the city be allowed to attend. Not to be outdone, the High Kingdom had sent a handful of knights along with their entire council, and while the wolves of Belaria had just bid the monarchs farewell, they felt the need to match everyone's numbers as well.

And then of course...there was one vampire.

Just the one. His son was nowhere in sight.

"Where are we supposed to sit?" Seth asked under his breath, looking suddenly uneasy. The barrier of entry might have been lower than they'd thought, but under no circumstance did it extend to lesser members of an alpine pack. "Or should we stand? I can stay by the door—"

"Don't be ridiculous," Evie said with a lot more confidence than she felt. "We're the ones who started all of this. The rest of them are just hopping on board."

With the imperious expression befitting a future queen of the High Kingdom, she grabbed her friends by the wrists and cut right through the center of the crowd. They parted for her, just as they'd done for her grandmother, watching as she joined the rest of her family alongside a table that had been dragged into the center of the room. A table bedecked in a full-size, topographical map.

This is EXACTLY how I imagined it might be.

Evie flashed a quick smile at her parents, then stared in childlike fascination—resisting the urge to poke the tops of the snowy peaks. It was a *perfect* replica. The rivers, the castles, the woods. Some undervalued servant had even managed to procure sand to sprinkle along the Kreo desert.

What happens to this stuff when we're done? Do they put it in a closet until the next apocalypse?

As the room slowly filled to capacity, she took a step closer—leaning down to examine her mother's castle in the High Kingdom, trying to find her room.

"My lord."

She glanced up quickly as a fae commander wove through the crowd to Cassiel, kneeling in a respectful bow with a fist clasped to the opposite shoulder. There were many such officers milling about the room, but this one appeared to be special. Cassiel stepped forward immediately and pulled him right back to his feet—embracing him with a warm smile.

"Aerin." He pulled back to look at him. "I wasn't sure you were coming."

"I still have a company of archers at my disposal," the fae replied with a teasing smile. "Do not be tricked by rumor." His bright eyes drifted to the map, lingering on a specific place high in the western mountains. "And let me assure you, they are quite keen to get back in the fight."

Cassiel followed his gaze, looking abruptly troubled.

"When I heard of..." He trailed off, unable to find the words. "I could never expect—"

"Your boy has come home," Aerin interrupted quietly, gazing across the table at the newly returned prince. "And look at all he brings with him. We are made whole by it, Cassiel."

The two men stared at each other a moment, then Cassiel gestured to Tanya with a smile.

"You remember...?"

"Of course." The fae bent down to kiss her hand. "My lady."

Evie was still watching, when a familiar voice sounded behind her.

"You'd think we could have done this much sooner."

Atticus Gail had been just a handful of times to the Ivory City, but to know a place a wolf only needed to go there once. Still, it was an unusual circumstance and he stayed close to his king's side. The same king who'd brought with him so many unusual circumstances when he'd returned home from years of travel himself. Retreating to his wife's castle in the High Kingdom, befriending dwarves and giants, flying off on the wings of a dragon and vanishing into the skies. Such was not the way of the pack. But the times had changed. Belaria had changed with them.

...to a point.

"You'd also think we could have done it in Belaria. But heaven forbid the Fae are required to leave their homes. Perhaps Kaleb Grey will be kind enough to bring the fight right here to Taviel."

Dylan flashed a faint smile. "I'm sorry, Atticus. Did the portal not agree with you?"

The councilman gave him a hard look. "Heaven forbid we travel by ship..."

At some unseen cue, a flood of servants entered the room—removing drinks and shuttering windows. The doors were closing and those who'd gathered were settling down.

How does that even happen?

Evie liked to think it involved a gong, or a burst of flaming arrows. Perhaps someone was ritually sacrificed and dangled from the ceiling by a spear.

She looked eagerly around the room, deciding who she'd want it to be.

Most of the people she saw gathered had never been to Taviel. Most of them would never be invited again. But these were special circumstances, and they needed to pull together.

And speaking of...

The doors opened a final time and Asher walked into the room.

He made no effort to announce himself, nor did he pay any attention to those who'd looked up in surprise. Those dark eyes swept the chamber for only a moment before he swept briskly down the center of the aisle and came to stand at his father's side.

Ellanden stared with quiet desperation, trying to catch his eye.

Evie stared deliberately at her shoes.

Who will begin the meeting?

For the first time, she noticed the empty spaces around the table where two people would have sat. Two people who'd been sitting around such tables for more centuries than perhaps anyone in the Ivory City except the oldest of fae.

Michael. Petra.

She shot a quick glance at her father and saw the color rising in his cheeks. No one had yet told her the full story of what transpired between them, but by the end of it both had ended up on separate mountains—exiled with varying degrees of guilt from the blissful world they used to know.

Why did no one send for them, she wondered, glancing around the room. *This isn't the time for old grudges—the realm is under attack. Where is our general? Where is our guide?*

Then a hush fell over the room and Kailas Damaris pushed to his feet.

"People of the realm...we thank you for coming."

Evie stared in shock as he began pacing in a slow circle, the entire citadel hanging on his every word. But the longer she sat there watching, the more it made perfect sense.

When their parents had fled the kingdoms, the weight of an empire had fallen squarely upon the prince's shoulders. He and his lovely wife. Together, they had navigated the aftermath as best they could. Guiding their people through the turbulent years that followed. Watching that empire splinter into a thousand pieces, then holding those pieces together with both hands.

They had ridden at the front of armies, proving themselves through feats of astonishing bravery and heartbreaking restraint. They had provided wise counsel and played cool politics, filling the thrones of six people though they were only two.

Kailas, in particular, was a natural choice.

Prince of the Fae by marriage, Crown Prince of the High Kingdom by birth. Brother-in-law to the heirs of both the Kreo and the Belarian thrones.

Evie studied him appraisingly.

Perhaps he could simply marry himself. Save me and Ellanden a lot of grief.

"—why there isn't any time left to waste," he concluded, coming to stand once more behind his chair. "For years we have watched the darkness slowly encroach upon our lands—never knowing the reason behind it. For years our sons and daughters have been on a quest to stop it, risking their lives as they toiled in secret, never knowing it had a name."

At that point, he gestured suddenly behind him.

"Evie...would you share with them the prophecy?"

She stared back at him, lips parting in surprise. It had been enough of a shock that she'd been admitted to such a meeting. Never had she dreamed she'd be required to speak.

But the question he was asking...she wasn't sure how she felt about it.

"Only if you wish," Katerina inserted quietly, looking into her daughter's eyes. "Only if you feel as though you should. But you have our assurances, the words will never leave this room."

Her voice rose in volume for the last bit, echoing to the back of the chamber. A quiet murmur of assent was soon to follow as those gathered leaned closer to hear the witch's words.

Should I tell them?

If she'd missed them before, how she longed for Michael and Petra now. Her eyes swept quickly around the little table before falling upon two young men.

Two men who'd set out with her at the beginning of the journey.

Two men who weren't currently speaking, but would risk their lives all the same.

For a suspended moment, the rest of the chamber faded away and it was only the three of them. There were no engagements or alliances, no threats or broken promises, none of the painful grievances that had driven them apart. Just three young friends nearing the end of their adventure, wondering what the next adventure might have in store...

"Tell them," Asher said quietly, staring into her eyes.

Ellanden glanced at him, then nodded.

"They have a right to know."

The princess nodded as well then turned to face the people, echoing those fateful words she'd heard so long ago. From a carnival tent in the High Kingdom, all the way to the Ivory City.

"Three shall set out, though three shall not return
To recover a stone from a land that won't burn.

Long they shall travel, for deep does it dwell
To bring to the land either heaven or hell.
They shall fall out of step in a land without time
And toil in shadow where stars cannot shine.
Old enemies prowl, for the dead never die
But peace will prevail if the dragon can fly."

A room full of the most powerful people in the land, but there was nothing but silence. Even their own parents, who'd heard the prophecy before, were hanging in its spell.

There was a fleeting moment when her eyes bypassed the people she knew best and went to the people she trusted the most. The oldest and the wisest. Leonor and Gran.

If one of them had said it was nonsense, she would have believed them. If one of them had said she'd been taken for a fool and shattered the realm for nothing, she would have gone back to her chamber in shame. But different as they were, both were staring with the exact same expression.

As if the words that came next belonged only to her.

"So you see why we left," she said quietly, somehow trusting the words would carry, "and you see why it's taken us so long to get back. We have been told what's happened in our absence, and for that we are eternally sorry. But the darkness you've tasted was already on its way."

Ellanden stood up beside her, but didn't say a word. On the other side of the table Asher stood as well, his dark eyes reflecting the faint glimmer of that sprawling map.

"The stone of which the fates have spoken lies somewhere in the Dunes. For years we have been searching, but were trapped in a heavy enchantment. We awoke to a land divided and a people already lost in despair. We must put that aside. We must gather our forces and march upon that wretched land. For we are not the only ones searching. Kaleb Grey is searching as well."

There was a sudden movement at the back of the room, and the princess lifted her eyes to see that her grandmother had decided to attend the meeting after all. She was standing in the very back, her eyes full of tears, but when she looked upon the princess she nodded her consent.

"He is not a man," Evie continued softly, "but a sorcerer. Part-wizard, part-dragon. And he is also looking for the stone. Whoever finds it first will have the power to dictate what happens next, and under no circumstance can that person be him. Unlike its twin, safeguarded by my mother, this is a dark stone. My friends and I intend to destroy it. Kaleb intends to use it for his own gain."

Just like that, the story was over. The secret the three of them had shared for over ten years was in the open, for everyone to hear. She stood there a moment longer, wondering if she should say anything else, then she sank back into her chair, feeling as though she'd run a great distance.

Dylan stared at her a moment, his eyes bright with pride. Then he pushed to his feet.

"We are to make for the High Kingdom with greatest speed, assembling the rest of the army to march in full force upon the Dunes. Ravens have already been sent. The troops are gathering. All that remains are the logistics of the search...and whatever forces Kaleb may have gathered himself."

At these words, the meeting abruptly finished.

Everyone gathered in the citadel pushed to their feet as a hundred conversations broke out all at once. Captains were conferring with their lieutenants, elders were giving out commands.

It was very controlled sort of chaos...and Evie went straight for her mother.

"I can't believe that just happened," she breathed, forgetting about appearances and leaning hard into her side. No one was watching anyway. The only people who gave her a second glance did so only to nod in solidarity before continuing on their way. "I can't believe I just said all that."

Katerina wrapped a strong arm around her shoulders, kissing the top of her head.

"I can."

They stood together beside the map, watching as the room swelled in volume as the doors opened and more people swept inside. It was as though the entire realm had been poised on a bed of tinder, just waiting for that fateful spark.

"Why are we going to the High Kingdom?" Evie asked suddenly.

Katerina glanced down in surprise. "What do you mean?"

"Well, I know we need a place on the mainland for the armies to rally before heading to the Dunes. Our strength is in numbers and we must all arrive together." Evie paused uncertainly. "But the High Kingdom isn't the most natural place for such a thing. Why not choose Liev or Nanorat, or some other city on the coast?"

Katerina stared at her a moment before bowing her head.

"I know your betrothal is an alliance, and your marriage is a treaty...but my daughter is still getting married," she said softly. "I thought we might have the wedding in your childhood home."

Evie froze in complete astonishment—it was the last thing in the world she expected her mother to say. But as small as the gesture was, considering the eternal weight of what she was about to do...just the thought of being home again brought tears to her eyes.

"Thank you," she whispered, closing the distance between them and throwing her arms around her mother's neck. "Thank you for that."

Katerina closed her eyes, silent tears spilling down her cheeks.

"Thank *you* for all of this," she answered softly. "You've saved us, Evie. If you hadn't left that day, if you hadn't received the prophecy..."

They pulled back a few inches, fresh tears on their faces. But before the princess could answer, a quiet voice caught her attention.

"Asher."

Ellanden had detached himself from the rest of them, trying to stop his friend before he vanished into the crowd. He closed the distance between them, reaching for the vampire's sleeve.

"Asher, could we—"

There was a blur of movement, followed by a quiet crack.

Seven hells!

Asher never stopped moving. He simply broke the fae's hand.

Chapter 11

"That son of a bitch!"

By the time Evie got to the prince's room, it was already full. Not in people so much, but in strength of conviction. While Seth was sitting rather mildly on the bed, Cosette's fiery indignation was enough for a company of grown men.

"It's not a big deal," Ellanden said for the tenth time, rubbing his eyes as Evie slipped into the room. "Would you please tell her it's not a big deal? Then maybe you could get her to leave?"

In the political nonsense that had unfolded upon reaching Taviel, the friends had remained largely neutral—mostly because while some of them may have been labeled the instigators, not one of them had escaped the heartbreak that had ensued. But Cosette apparently drew the line at physical violence, because she was perched on her cousin's bed like a snake poised to spring.

"She will do no such thing!" she hissed, glaring at the door as if waiting for the vampire to suddenly arrive. "The nerve of him! Like marrying Ellanden is *anything* Evie would actually want!"

The three of them cast the fae an unseen look before turning back to their separate corners.

Not helping.

Evie drifted to the prince's side, stifling a grimace.

His hand wasn't just broken, it had been shattered beyond belief. Just a flick of the vampire's fingers, but the delicate bones had snapped straight through the center.

In a perfect world, he would have been complaining. But since Cosette was complaining enough for the both of them, he was painfully holding his tongue.

"It's fine," he said preemptively. "Honestly, I shouldn't...I shouldn't have grabbed for him."

"Are you *apologizing*?!" Cosette shrieked.

He banged his head against the wall behind him.

"*Please*...make her leave."

"I can get you some ice," Seth offered, grimacing as well when he looked down at the fae's hand. "But you should probably see a healer. That kind of thing won't mend on its own."

Ellanden shook his head dismissively.

"It's *fine*. If you could all just—"

There was a knock on the door.

The four friends turned at the same time, staring in silence, then Ellanden shot a sarcastic glance at his cousin. "It's the keeper at the asylum. He's come for your soul."

Her eyes narrowed dangerously.

"I'm going to *kill* you, then fix your hand."

He grinned in spite of himself, glancing at Seth.

"Make careful note: this is the girl to whom you've pledged yourself."

The door knocked again.

"Come in."

The friends glanced up as it opened, then froze abruptly still.

Seven hells.

Aidan stepped inside without a word of greeting, sparing not a glance for the rest of them as his dark eyes fixed upon Ellanden's hand. He stared a moment, then looked at the fae himself.

Many years before, when the children were little, both boys had gone with the vampire on a camping trip. It hadn't been planned, they'd simply strayed ahead of the rest of the group. But the evening before they were supposed to reconvene the ground gave out on the ledge where Ellanden had been standing, and he toppled without a hope or prayer over the top of the mountainside.

Asher had cried out in terror, too small to do a thing to stop it. Aidan had turned more slowly, his mind focused on something else, just in time to see the little fae vanish over the side.

It could have been the end of him, but his uncle caught his hand.

Never would the princess forget how they'd looked when they hiked back fourteen miles and limped into their families' campsite. Asher had been a wreck with worry and Ellanden had been asleep in his uncle's arms. Blood all over his face. Blood all over Aidan's face. Young, immortal blood. But still, the fae clung to him. Oblivious of the temptation, of the sacrifice underwritten into each vampiric step. Aidan held on to him gently, whispering soft comforts the whole way.

Ellanden would trust his uncle with his life.

But in that solitary moment...he wasn't entirely sure.

"I'm sorry," he apologized on instinct, taking a step towards the bed. "I wasn't trying to provoke him..."

That's when the healer stepped inside.

The friends closed their eyes in embarrassment, relaxing their rigid posture as the medic crossed quickly to the prince's side. Ironic as it was, the man was fae. Despite however long he'd been away, Aidan Dorsett still had quite a bit of clout in the Ivory City.

"It's most definitely broken," the healer murmured under his breath. "Several times." Of all the people in the room, he was the only one not to have been present in the citadel. "What happened?"

There was a beat of silence.

"An accident," Ellanden said quickly, shooting a preemptive look at Cosette. "I was being too rough."

The man's eyes flickered towards him before he took a step back. "I can fix it slowly, or all at once."

"Please." The prince extended it without hesitation. "Just set it and be done."

Evie's stomach tightened and she looked away as the healer braced the young fae against the bed and pulled the bones back into place.

Crack. Ellanden let out a soft cry, muffling it in his other arm as best he could. Aidan watched every moment, a look of indescribable sadness on his face.

"There...can you move any fingers?"

Ellanden clenched his jaw, then flexed them as best he could.

The doctor studied every motion, then stepped back with a brisk nod. "That's very good, but do nothing further tonight. The longer you rest, the faster it will heal. No archery, no riding."

Who would he shoot? Where would he go?

Evie wondered both questions in silence, but such general restrictions were apparently rather standard for a fae. Ellanden nodded swiftly, making a show of reclining back upon the bed.

"Thank you," the vampire murmured, dismissing the man with a wave of his hand. He stared instead at the prince, waiting until the door was closed. "Ellanden...I'm so very sorry."

"Please," the fae countered quickly, shaking his head, "don't."

A charged silence fell between them, full of apology and so much more.

No one else seemed to know where to look. If Asher himself had returned, it couldn't have been worse than his soft-spoken father. A man who'd felt the pain of that break a hundred times more than the rest of them. A man who'd opened the door with a healer at his side.

"You spoke well today," Aidan said abruptly, flashing Evie the hint of a smile. "I could tell you weren't expecting to say anything...but you did very well."

She flashed him a nervous look as the tension eased another few degrees. "I wasn't expecting to share the prophecy," she admitted. "The gist of it—of course. But not a direct recounting, quoting it word for word."

Aidan raked back his hair, looking suddenly tired. "I didn't want you to," he replied, "but Kailas insisted upon full transparency. He seemed to think the people deserved to hear it, and I cannot disagree with him on that count."

"But you *do* disagree," Seth prompted curiously. "Why?"

A few weeks ago, he would have been terrified to stay in the same room as the vampire let alone ask him a direct question. But Aidan had a way of chipping those barriers away.

"Prophecies are vague," he answered, "open to multiple interpretations. But this isn't a situation in which multiple opinions are helpful."

His eyes settled on Evie.

"The prophecy was given to *you*. That only opinion that matters is yours."

For perhaps the first time since the night of the carnival, the princess would have given anything she had for that *not* to be the case. She didn't want to bear the weight of it alone, to feel responsible for every broken promise and twist of the knife that had happened since they'd left.

There was no end to it.

The grim expression on Aidan's face, lost brothers at Cadarest, the fae's broken hand. There wasn't a single recent tragedy that couldn't be tied to some decision she'd personally made.

Her gaze drifted out the window towards the gleaming citadel.

...and now this.

"I'll leave you to rest," Aidan said quietly, backing away at the same time. "And do not ignore the advice of the healer, Ellanden. There must be no strenuous activity with that hand."

Seth pawed innocently at the floor with his boot.

"You're in for a different kind of night."

The fae hurled a pillow at him, leaving his long-suffering cousin to insert herself quickly in between, while Evie left the others and shadowed after her uncle into the hall.

"Where is he?"

Aidan paused, then turned slowly around. "I will speak to him about—"

"Uncle...*please*. Tell me where he is."

The vampire folded his arms, then cocked his head towards the patio.

...thank you.

She was gone in a flash, racing at full speed down the corridor, hoping she could get there before he vanished. He must have been lingering deliberately within ear shot, checking up on Ellanden, otherwise he never would have been so close to begin with.

Because he knows it was wrong. Because he knows what a giant MONSTER he's been.

Sure enough, Asher was poised in the center of the patio—tilting his head towards the villa, listening with such intense concentration that he didn't see his girlfriend barreling towards him.

...until she'd pushed him over the balcony.

"Evie," he gasped in astonishment, somehow managing to land on his feet. By the time he glanced up, she'd leapt over the side herself and landed right behind him. "What are you...?"

He trailed into silence, staring in utter shock.

"You're angry with me?"

Bingo.

Strangely enough, it wasn't the fall over the railing that clued him in. Since they were just children, his high-spirited friends tended to express themselves in such a way.

It was the bond.

"You are, I can't believe it," he murmured in amazement. "*You're* angry with *me*."

If she'd had a stick, the princess would have clubbed him.

"Congratulations, Ash. You've solved it."

His eyes flashed, but he maintained a perfect calm.

"Is that why you're here?" he quipped. "Are you avenging him?"

She took a step closer, literally trembling with rage.

"Am I avenging him?" she answered slowly, emphasizing each word. "You're a smart guy, Asher. Use complete sentences like you were taught. Am I *confronting* the man who attacked his best friend and broke half the bones in his hand? Yes, that's *precisely* what I'm doing."

A muscle twitched in the back of his jaw. "The healer said he'd be fine—"

She slapped him across the face.

"So will you."

He lifted a hand to his cheek, glaring beneath a veil of dark hair.

"You have no right to be angry—"

"You *left* me, Asher!" she shouted. "You *promised* you would never do that!"

"And you promised yourself to another!"

The two of them were standing toe to toe, yelling like the world was on fire, while the garden around them was eerily quiet and still.

"You walked into that room and promised to marry someone else!" he cried. "After everything that's happened between us! The prophecy, the bond! I told you I *love* you! Do you know how rare that is?! That a person like me would be able to fall in love?!"

He turned away suddenly, glaring back tears.

"You know what the worst part is? The moment right before, when you were making your little speech about securing alliances through marriage, I actually thought..."

He shook his head, pulling in a fractured breath.

"What does it matter? You made the decision for both of us. It's over now, it's done." He squared his shoulders. "As soon as I've fulfilled my role in the prophecy, I can finally be rid of this place. You and Ellanden can ride off together into the sunset. You'll never have to see me again—"

"Are you *listening* to what you're *saying*?!" She raised a hand to slap him again, but it dropped back to her side.

He stared at her, mouth open.

"You think I *want* this?! You think I *want* to get married to a man I don't love?! Why am I even asking the bloody question, Asher? You *know* I don't! You can feel it through the bond—"

"You have a hilarious way of showing it," he interrupted, eyes blazing into hers. "Proposing to my brother on a spontaneous whim? Promising yourself to him for all eternity—"

"ON PAPER!" she screamed. "TO SAVE PEOPLE'S LIVES!"

A sudden silence rang between them, but the princess couldn't let it stand.

"I saw what needed to be done, I saw it was our only option—and I took the bloody initiative to get it done! At *great* personal cost! Why must I be the one to constantly apologize?!"

Most people would have backed off, but the vampire wasn't most people.

"You consulted no one! You spoke with no one! I was standing right beside you, and you didn't say a thing!" He paced a few steps away, trying to rein in his anger, then whirled back around. "If I'd known something like this would happen, I never would have let us fly back to our parents. We could have been in the forest right now, same as we'd been the last ten years. And nothing would have been different. And everything could have carried on just the same—"

"And everyone we loved would soon be dead!"

He leapt back suddenly as a burst of dragon fire poured from her hands. It spilled onto the ground between them, melting a permanent line into the ancient stone.

They stared from opposite sides before lifting their eyes to each other.

"I understand that you're angry," she said quietly, arms shaking by her sides. "I understand how it feels to have an entire future ripped straight out of your hands. But you're not the one who has to sleep with someone you don't want. Someone who doesn't want you."

She stared at him a moment longer, then stormed back inside.

"You're not the one who has four kingdoms telling you to take off your dress."

EVIE STAYED IN HER bedroom for the rest of the day, watching in secret as a pair of servants tried their best to remove the line of scorched ivory from the patio stone. It was a valiant attempt, but there were few things as powerful as dragon fire. In the end they shared a silent look, then one of them simply covered the evidence with a potted plant.

The second they left, she wandered back outside herself—tilting her face to the sky and leaning over the railing. There were voices in the courtyard below her. Ellanden and Cosette had apparently reconciled and were taking advantage of those last few hours of sun.

"—never said that directly," the prince was saying. "Only that you might want to reconsider devoting your life to someone so completely devoid of higher thought."

"It's not his first language," Cosette threw up her hands in exasperation. "I think it's sweet he's making an effort to learn—"

"An effort," Ellanden repeated doubtfully. "It sounded like he was having a fit."

The woodland princess turned her face, unable to keep from smiling.

"Perhaps we should take him to the healer," her cousin suggested enthusiastically. "See if anything can be done. I'd be more than happy to arrange such a thing myself, especially if the idea makes you uncomfortable—"

A crackling voice made Evie jump.

"Quite the charmer...your betrothed."

She glanced over in alarm, then made a conscious effort not to flinch. No matter how many times she saw that sunken face, she didn't think she'd ever get used to it.

Betrothed.
The word was so jarring, it didn't even register.

"I'm sorry?"

She tensed in dismay as Melkins leaned beside her against the railing, peering down into the courtyard below. "Your future husband. It's a good match," he added. "One of my best."

She let out a quiet sigh.

"You don't think so?"

For the first time, she wondered if he cared. Not that it would make much of a difference, but it might imply a bit of a soul inside that withered shell.

When she didn't answer, he glanced once more at the fae.

"He's handsome, intelligent, charismatic. A talented statesman, a gifted warrior. You've known him all your life, I've seen him make you smile." He tilted his head curiously, trying to catch her gaze. "Is it a matter of fidelity? Do you not think he'll make a good father?"

Her breathing hitched and she followed his gaze.

Of course, the point of such a marriage. To make an heir.

As she stared down from the balcony her mind drifted back to that day they'd spent with the Kreo, when Asher had broken things off and Ellanden had comforted her in the meadow. He'd already been there when she'd arrived, playing with the village children.

Despite all they'd just been through, the image was a happy one.

He'd put his bow away, the shipwreck was forgotten. There were children dripping off his arms and he was breathless with laughter, spinning them round and round in the sun.

"Ellanden will make a wonderful father," she answered softly.

He just wasn't the father she'd had in mind.

They watched in silence for a while longer, staring unnoticed from behind the branches of the flowering trees, then she turned to the carionelle with sudden curiosity.

"You said that Ellanden reminded you of someone...whatever happened to him?"

The ancient matchmaker glanced over in surprise before turning back to the courtyard.

"He fell in love with someone else," he said simply, lips twitching in a wry smile. "And quite a match it was. He never married. One of the only people to escape my net."

Evie found herself smiling without knowing the reason why. "You must resent him...he got the fairytale."

Melkins shook his head with a distant expression. "I don't resent him," he said softly. "In fact, I rather admire him."

He stared a moment longer, then headed back inside.

"Few people get the fairytale, Your Highness. And as for that man..." His gaze rose to the darkening sky. "...I never saw him again."

Chapter 12

Evie paced back and forth in her chambers, straying occasionally to the balcony to watch the preparations unfolding in the city below. Most of them were rather straightforward, considering the present situation. Spare weapons and armor were being packed into crates for transport. Rations of food and medicinal supplies were gathered from the forest and boxed up next. Despite the inherent tranquility of their surroundings, the people of the Ivory City were readying themselves for war.

...and a wedding.

Those who weren't carrying blades were armed with flowers. And while some were stacking quivers of arrows in the corner, others were marching past them with armfuls of candles, calling out instructions to one another as they made their way to and from the citadel.

It was the princess' last night on foreign soil.

In the morning everyone gathered in Taviel would travel to the mainland, where they would unite with the rest of the realm, conduct the ceremony, and march off to war.

If it's an actual a war. If Kaleb's gathered an actual army to fight.

Strange as it was, there was still no technical proof that he'd done such a thing. The waves of darkness that fractured the land were gradual and insidious, gaining strength through discourse and discontent. They crept closer by chipping away at protections, then empowering creatures that had been hunted to near extinction. Preying first upon those in isolation before working towards the cities, then into the council rooms themselves. It was more of an infection than a sudden assault.

Although, if the man *wanted* to rally an army...he had plenty to choose from.

Just a few hours earlier, Evie had watched in fascination as a company of fae warriors swept past carrying what looked like several small trees between them. At first, she thought it was a bizarre team-building exercise or an ill-timed construction project gone awry. She'd mentioned as much to Leia when she came with a noontime tray, but was corrected with a simple, "It's for the giants."

The princess had stopped asking questions after that, though she continued her silent vigil.

Giants, trolls, demons, Carpathians...there seemed no end to the nightmarish things her uncle could assemble to fight alongside him. All those twisted evils he'd allowed to take root.

In a moment of quiet terror, she wondered if the vampires might join him as well.

They had always been erratic when it came to choosing sides in such unilateral conflicts, often preferring to simply avoid them instead. In addition to a general lack of conscience, they had a deep-rooted aversion to any fight they weren't already certain they could win. Rational arguments and speeches of honor could never persuade them to align themselves with a losing side.

But not everyone is as savage as they were before.

The princess thought of the community living in secret within the mountains—the oldest and most respected of their kind. She thought of the nearby village of 'companions' that had been attacked in a raid, how the vampires in question had come without hesitation to their defense.

But most of them don't choose to live in such a manner. And Diana told me herself that the fulfillment of the prophecy may be the end of her people. That's not a risk she'd be willing to take.

These were the issues preoccupying the princess. Much easier to speculate about fire and brimstone than to face the more immediate reality of what was about to happen.

Because before there could be war, there must first be marriage.

Maybe I can slip away tonight, she thought to herself, leaning wistfully over the balcony. *Stretch my wings one final time before the chains of matrimony. Or I could avoid the portal and just fly—*

The second she thought the word, it was as if some higher power took control of her body and abandoned all higher thought. Her dress was quickly discarded, her shoes were soon to follow, and before she could even consider what she was doing she'd thrown her body over the side of the balcony, plummeting with deadly speed towards the courtyard—

—before rising again in a burst of dragon fire.

THIS is more like it!

With a cry of delight the princess unfurled her wings and soared upwards, leaving the island altogether as she vanished into the canopy of wispy clouds. It was a freedom unlike any she'd ever known, one that made her suddenly realize how caged she'd felt in the lovely villa down below.

From such a great distance, the people themselves had vanished and the famed city looked like a child's toy. The expensive kind. The kind one would only be allowed to play with under the careful supervision of a governess. The polished streets faded to nothing more than a dull gleam and the glinting towers of the ivory citadel grew small upon the horizon as she glided over the waves.

I could just keep going, she thought with sudden abandon, pumping her powerful wings as she skimmed the top of the sea. *I could leave it all behind me.*

The princess in her agreed immediately, but she was tempered by the future queen. Those people in the citadel were gathering candles for a reason. Those people in the armory were gathering arrows for a reason. And there were men and women all over the realm doing the exact same thing.

We just need to get through these next couple of days. Just a few more days, then we can go to the Dunes with a massive army, find the stone, and annihilate whoever stands in our way. Just a few more days—

She stopped herself suddenly, eyes flying back to the island.

But it isn't just a few more days, it's everything that comes after.

Even if she managed to get through the wedding without fainting, even if she managed to fulfill the prophecy without getting herself killed...she couldn't begin to fathom the things that came next.

In a kind of daze, she thought back to the day before they'd set off on their grand adventure, all those years ago. The day she'd scaled the castle walls to tell Ellanden about the prophecy, and then ended up having to hide from the royal bodyguards inside his bed.

Tangling with him beneath the sheets, her cheek pressed against the smooth muscles of his stomach...everything about it felt awkward and wrong. And again, at the Kreo village. Never could she forget when he'd leaned suddenly towards her, crushing his mouth to hers. When he'd lowered her onto the bed, her first and only instinct had been to punch him. Granted, that wasn't actually Ellanden. It was a shape-shifter, playing a prank. But that didn't matter, she believed it was him.

And just the thought of it...the idea of the two of us...when the time comes for us to actually...

She tilted precariously towards the ocean.

I can't do this!

AS QUICKLY AS SHE'D tried to flee, the princess circled back to the Ivory City—desperate to shed the scales and pull in a human breath. The logistics of landing in such a place were difficult under the best of circumstances, but it was nothing compared to the nudity after the fact. It was the kind of thing she'd usually have kept in mind—touching down on the edge of her balcony, then darting inside before anyone could see. Except the princess wasn't thinking, she was panicking.

And she didn't land on her balcony.

She landed on the fae's instead.

Thinking back on it later, it was lucky Ellanden was even there. Between the war and wedding, there seemed to be an unending list of things to do. But the fae avoided such logistical quagmires the same way she did herself, though he clearly didn't trust himself to be alone with his own thoughts. When she crash-landed on his balcony, the Prince of the Fae was reading a book.

He wasn't at the desk or the table, although there was plenty of room for such a thing. He wasn't even sitting on one of the numerous chairs, but had wedged himself between the bed and the bookcase, resting his chin absentmindedly in his hand with a novel splayed in front of him.

By the time he glanced up, the dragon had vanished and only the girl remained. Their eyes met and he smiled sweetly, too distracted to immediately notice what was wrong.

Then it clicked.

"What the hell are you doing?!"

The words blended into a single breathless gasp as the fae leapt to his feet—covering his eyes whilst streaking across the room to unlock the door. The combination was slightly disastrous.

"Seven hells!" He tripped over a decorative fountain with a curse, spilling buckets of water across the floor. "Did you just shift or something? What's the matter with you?!"

"I have to talk to you," Evie gasped, fingers tapping anxiously on the door. The panic had taken hold so completely she was unable to properly speak. "I can't do this. We can't—"

"Get inside," he commanded, grabbing her arm and yanking her out of sight.

The door swung shut behind her and he hastily averted his gaze, looking in absolutely every direction except where she was standing, trying to remember where he'd left his cloak.

"Where the hell are your clothes?" He finally just grabbed a blanket, extending it blindly between them. "You can't just show up like that, Evie! What if someone had—"

"You can't even look at me!"

The room went suddenly silent.

The two of them stood there, not moving, not breathing, without having the faintest idea of what to say. The blanket hung between them like a wilted flag, growing heavier with each second.

"How are we supposed to...?" She shook her head in desperation, wild tears flying off her cheeks. "How are we supposed to get *married*, when you can't even look at me?"

He froze where he was standing, looking suddenly pale. "I...I don't know."

It was that faltering honesty that derailed her, that broke through the hysteria, letting her calm down enough to grab the blanket and wrap it miserably around her shoulders.

Suddenly, it didn't matter how much progress they'd been making. It didn't matter how many years had passed, or how many leagues they'd crossed to get to that point.

There was no escaping this one simple thing.

"Let me get your clothes."

He was out the door before she could lift her head, returning just a few seconds later with the pile of things she'd dropped before taking flight. She put them on in silence, fingers trembling beyond control. He stared deliberately in the opposite direction, waiting until she was finished.

"I can't believe this is happening," she murmured. "Of all the things to..." She trailed off, shaking her head. "Asher hates me, by the way. So that's over before it began."

Good thing we decided to bond for all eternity.

Ellanden stared back in silence, his broken hand throbbing at his side.

"Freya hates me, too," he finally managed. "I thought we might be able to...but I've been assured that's finished. She told Cosette that she's leaving."

The princess looked up in shock.

"...when?"

"Once we get back to the mainland," he answered quietly, staring at the ripples of water pooling on the floor. "She said the prophecy was never about her anyway, and now that we have four separate armies behind us she doesn't see the value in adding one witch."

Doesn't see the value?

Evie sucked in a quick breath, feeling as if the world was unravelling.

"But it isn't...it isn't safe!" she cried, latching on to the easiest thing. "The entire realm is preparing for battle and she wants to head off on her own? Where would she even go? Harenthall is weeks away by foot—"

"She's not going to Harenthall. She's going to Vale." He sank on to the bed, running a tired hand through his hair. "She asked my Gran to make her a portal, once everything is settled."

The princess opened her mouth, then closed it again. In a way, it made perfect sense. Vale was a territory, one of the few places left in the realm where Freya's ex-boyfriend wasn't a member of the ruling family. Instead of coming up with anything clever to say, she settled for a simple, "...oh."

It was quiet for a few seconds longer.

"Asher's only staying until it's finished." She turned her face quickly, wiping away tears with the back of her hand. "After the Dunes...I don't think I'll ever see him again."

Ellanden stared in painful silence, then dropped his eyes to the floor. "I don't know what I expected," he admitted softly. "It wasn't like they could stay."

The fae was right. Had she really expected anything different? Would her own parents have continued to see each other if they'd been forced into such an arrangement themselves? She wanted to say yes—if nothing else, they'd been commanded to marry different siblings of the same ancient family. No doubt their paths would have crossed. But deep down, she knew the answer.

They wouldn't have been able to bear it. Not when they'd loved each other so fiercely. They would have spent all their time in different kingdoms, living on opposite sides of the map. To even glimpse each other after they'd taken vows would have been—

That part is out of your control, she steadied herself. *But the immediate problem remains.*

She took a deep breath, then crossed the room and took his non-injured hand—pulling him back to his feet. "How can we get married, if you can't even look at me?"

He tensed involuntarily, but she held on tight.

"This whole day I've been watching people get ready from the balcony, thinking we just need to get through it. We just need to get through the ceremony, then everything will be okay."

She stared up at him, nothing but raw honesty.

"But that's just the beginning of it, Ellanden. The foundation of everything else that's going to come. And if we can't figure out how to make it work...*nothing* is going to be okay."

He nodded silently, but couldn't meet her eyes. "I know that. And we will figure it out, I promise. It's just—"

"You're going to be my husband," she said softly. "I'm going to be your wife." She gave a deliberate weight to the words, letting each one resonate. It was time to stop running. It was time to face them. "The wedding's tomorrow and the alliance is at stake. We need to get past this."

Come hell or high water...

She lifted a hand to his cheek, then stretched onto her toes.

At the last possible second, he realized what she was about to do. A breath caught in his chest and he pulled away in surprise, wrapping his fingers around her wrists.

"Evie—"

"It's just me," she whispered. "And it's just you."

And we had better get used to that.

His eyes tightened painfully, staring over her head.

Help him. This was your idea, help him through it.

"You promised you'd never make me beg," she said lightly, trying her best to smile. Humor was usually a safe bet. "Is it the occasional scales? The dragon fire? Am I not pretty—"

"Of course you are," he assured her, clasping her hands, "you know you are. I've always thought so." His dark eyes locked on hers, enormous and unsure. "Evie...this will break us."

Yes, it will.

She pulled in a deep breath, then said the only thing she could.

"This will *save* everyone."

It was impossible to lie to a fae. It was even more impossible to lie to her best friend. But on this one excruciating point, she happened to be telling the truth.

"We need..." She shook her head with a sigh. "Landi, we need to get past this."

Their eyes met for a suspended moment. Then she kissed him.

It felt...wrong.

Like kissing a brother. Like kissing a statue. That second one wasn't too far off, because the fae had gone absolutely rigid the moment they touched. He hadn't even pulled in a breath.

She leaned back, lips twitching with a sarcastic grin.

"...that was incredible."

He laughed in spite of himself, letting it all out in one breath. It lingered on his face as he stared down at her, catching a lock of hair and tucking it affectionately behind her ear.

The laughter helped. So would the whiskey.

She spotted the remainder of their bottle on his shelf and poured them two glasses. Half of hers was gone in a single gulp, but when she offered the other to him he put them both away.

"You don't want anything?" she asked in confusion.

He shook his head, placing the bottle back on the shelf.

"You're right," he said softly. "We need to get past this. But it's not going to be like..." He shook his head again, turning away from the whiskey. "I love you, Everly. Even if it's not...even if it's not the way that's required. I love you. That should be enough."

A shiver swept over her body. Her palms started tingling.

We're actually going to do this.

True to form, she started making things worse.

"This better be good," she joked nervously, "there's been a lot of hype."

He closed his eyes ever so briefly. "Please stop—"

"By hype, I mean women."

"I'm serious—"

"There have been a lot of women."

"*Everly.*"

They stared at each other, then they kissed again.

They went into it fast. Blind. Holding onto each other's faces for guidance with their eyes closed tight. Yes, it was strange. But after a few seconds, she was able to detach from that, erasing all emotion and existing only in the physicality. Yes, it was strange...but it was also good.

She stretched onto her toes, sliding her fingers into his hair. He stiffened involuntarily, then swept her abruptly off her feet, backing up until his legs were touching the edge of the mattress.

The bed suddenly looked enormous. They were both hyper-aware of it.

A wave of panic descended upon them, and Ellanden was about to suggest they drink some of that whiskey after all, when she pushed him suddenly onto his back, climbing on top.

His lips parted in surprise as he stared up at her, unsure of his next moves, unsure how far she wanted to go. He reached instinctively towards her, then stopped himself at the same time.

"Should we stop?" he asked, trying to catch his breath. "Do you want to stop?"

She froze above him, utterly paralyzed.

...what's the point?

They came to the realization at the same time, then forced themselves back together.

This time was different than before. More frantic. More urgent. She grabbed a fist of his hair. His tongue slipped into her mouth. She pulled open the lacing on his shirt, while his fingers trailed down her sides. They lingered a moment on her hips, then pulled her down towards him.

Clothes stretched and tore as things got faster. Their eyes shut again and they clasped themselves together—both thinking of other faces, both trying not to think at all.

She wrapped her legs around him. His hand slid slowly up dress—

"Seven hells."

He pulled back with a grimace. At least, he tried to. The braids in his hair had caught on her necklace—fastening them together with a row of sparkling white gems.

She reached up to unclasp it, then realized all at once what it was.

"What is it?" Ellanden panted. "Are you okay?"

...no.

Her eyes filled with tears as she removed it quickly—scooting to the far edge of the mattress as he reached up to untangle it himself.

"Asher gave that to me."

The room went dead still. All except the jewels swinging lightly in his hair.

"We should probably get some sleep."

"Have a lot to pack before tomorrow."

They spoke at the same time, shared a swift look, then turned away quickly—cheeks flaming in the fading light. In a flash the princess was off the bed, pacing across the room without daring to look back, while the fae was perfectly frozen, a strand of diamonds still knotted in his ivory hair.

"I'll see you tomorrow, Ellanden."

He glanced up quickly, nodding his head. "Yeah, I'll...I'll see you tomorrow."

Chapter 13

Time moved rather strangely for the rest of the night, lurching by in wild bursts before stalling out completely. Before Evie could catch up with what was happening the sun was simmering on the edge of the distant horizon, and there was a quiet knock on her door.

"Milady?" Leia's gentle voice drifted through. "I've come to help you get ready."

She blinked slowly at the ceiling.

By the end of today...I will be married.

They went quickly through the motions, speaking only when necessary. The ceremony wasn't until that evening, so there was no need to dress. The bulk of what they did was packing. The only awkward moment came when the fae asked if she'd like to wear her 'special necklace'.

The princess shook her head, eyes shining with tears. There was no more talking after that.

When at last they were finished the lovely woman stepped back to survey her work, then nodded with a satisfied smile. "Well...this is where I leave you, milady."

Evie's head snapped up in shock. "What do you mean? You're not...you're not coming with us to the High Kingdom?"

The fae shook her head. "Some people are needed to stay behind and defend Taviel, if the worst should happen."

If the worst should happen...Taviel won't stand a chance.

"Of course, I understand." Evie glanced swiftly at the floor, feeling unexpectedly shaken by the sudden farewell. "In that case, I wish you the best of luck—"

She broke off suddenly when the fae pressed a kiss to her cheek.

"Best of luck to *you*, milady." Her eyes twinkled with a smile. "Sweet child...do not lose yourself to despair. These things do not happen without a higher reason, even if you can't see it yet."

Evie stared in surprise, then threw her arms around the fae's neck.

NO SOONER HAD LEIA left than there was a faint crackling outside the princess' window, a metallic buzzing sound that she'd come to associate with magic and nausea. Sure enough, a blaze of neon sparks was already glinting from somewhere inside the citadel.

The portal was open. It was time to leave.

"Knock, knock." She turned around just as Dylan pushed open the door, eyeing her mountain of suitcases with a little smile. "Packing light, I see."

She lifted her shoulders in a shrug. "My father promised to carry them. I like to give him a challenge."

He laughed quietly before lifting his eyes to her face. "...how are you feeling?"

She tapped manically on her legs, feeling like she was about to pass out. "Fine. Totally fine."

He studied her a moment longer, then nodded slowly. "You seem totally fine."

"I am," she agreed. "*Totally* fine."

He cocked his head to the window. "You want me to create some kind of diversion? Start a forest fire?"

Her lips twitched in a reluctant grin. "Didn't this entire city once burn to the ground? That's really bad form—"

"Evie...how are you feeling?"

A sudden silence fell between them, punctuated only by the occasional hiss of sparks as another person stepped through the portal. After a minute, she gave another helpless shrug.

"Does it matter?"

He crossed the room in four quick strides, pulling her into a tight embrace.

"Of course it matters," he murmured, pressing a kiss to her hair. "Sweetheart...I know your reasons for doing this. And I couldn't be more proud that you volunteered. But just because this is the most practical solution doesn't mean—"

"Dad?"

She shook her head, flashing a watery smile.

"Can you just help me with the bags?"

TEN MINUTES LATER, the room was empty and the princess had officially run out of reasons to delay. While her father carried the last of her things down to the courtyard, she took a trembling breath and walked a final time to the balcony—wishing once again it was possible to simply fly away.

Strangely enough, it wasn't the prospect of the ceremony that night that was weighing most heavily on her mind. It was those fleeting moments that had happened the night before.

They kept coming back to her, one after another.

The feel of his chest beneath her fingers. The way her skin tickled as he kissed the hollow beneath her ear. The way it felt strange, and then...nothing.

Not a hint of conflict. Not a hint of emotion.

Not a hint of what I felt with Asher.

She gripped the banister, gazing vacantly at the portal.

Is that how it's going to be from now on? Will I just feel empty?

There was a quiet knock behind her.

"Yeah, I'm coming." She turned with a sigh as the door opened. "You got the last of the cases, Dad. I don't need—"

She froze dead still.

Asher.

The vampire was hovering uncertainly in the doorway, one hand still raised to knock. His eyes swept quickly over the room, stalling for time, then landing on the princess herself.

"...I wasn't sure you'd still be here," he admitted quietly.

She stared back with wide eyes, unable to move an inch.

"I could say the same thing about you."

A hint of color flushed his cheeks, and he dropped his gaze to the floor.

"Yeah, I've been...I've been thinking a lot about what you said."

Normally so eloquent, the vampire paused with a look of uncharacteristic helplessness, keeping those dark eyes fixed on the floor. A little tremor shook his hands, curling them into involuntary fists before he smoothed them deliberately flat upon his legs.

"You were right," he said abruptly. "Everything you said in the courtyard...you were right about all of it. I've known how this was since we were children. You're a princess, Ellanden's a prince. It was never going to..." He trailed off, starting again. "I love you, Evie. I'm going to spend the rest of my life loving you. I'm never going to come round to the idea of you marrying someone else. But I know that it wasn't *your* idea. And I...I have no right to be angry about that."

He bowed his head in defeat.

"I'm sorry I left," he said quietly. "I'm sorry I broke my promise. And I'm sorry I made you feel like it was your fault. Of course it wasn't. Nothing like this has ever been required of me. And you're right, I'm not the one who has to..."

Evie let out a silent breath, feeling like there was a sudden weight upon her chest.

How is this happening?

"Please—stop." She held up her hand before he could say anything else, feeling like she was going to faint right there on the floor. "You had every right to be angry, Asher. You still have every right to be angry. It isn't like—"

"I yelled at you," he interrupted softly. "I left you alone. After promising to always stand beside you, the first thing I did was to walk away. I broke Ellanden's hand..."

He closed his eyes, looking sick with himself.

"Like he wants this any more than you. Like he isn't crushed about Freya—"

"Please," she said again, holding a hand between them, "stop."

How is this be happening right now?!

"Asher, I love you all the more for saying that," she began shakily, "but you need to understand. This is more than just—"

There was another knock on the door.

"Evie?"

Her face went pale.

"Not now, Ellanden!"

But Asher was already opening the door. And the fae was already stepping inside. He froze dead still upon seeing them, closing the gems he was returning quickly in his hand.

"Sorry," he stammered, retreating back towards the hall, "I didn't mean to—"

"No, this is perfect," Asher interrupted, catching his shirt and pulling him gently forward. "I was just coming to find you. Landi...I'm sorry about your hand."

The fae glanced instinctively at the hidden necklace.

"My hand?" He looked up uncertainly, then caught Evie's pained expression. "Oh, my hand!" His face cleared with a look of utter relief before shadowing just as quickly. "It's fine, please don't apologize. The whole thing was my—"

But the vampire was on a roll.

"I'm serious," he insisted, "it's unacceptable. I should have tracked you down yesterday, but you were with the healer and I didn't...I didn't want..."

He trailed off with a strange expression, staring directly at the fae.

Asher?

Ellanden and Evie exchanged a quick look, then the fae backed away again.

"They're waiting for me by the portal," he said uncertainly, "I'm going to let you guys—"

But the vampire yanked him back again, still holding on to his shirt. There was a split second when nothing happened, then Asher wrapped a sudden hand around the back of his head.

Evie stepped forward in alarm. "What are you doing?"

It wasn't possible. It simply couldn't be happening.

"Asher, what are you doing?" Ellanden echoed warily, straining in spite of himself against the vampire's iron grip. "Let me—"

Asher leaned suddenly forward, sniffing his skin.

Oh, shit...

Ellanden made the connection at the same time, paling white as a ghost. The vampire wasn't thirsty at all, it was something far worse than that. He'd found his girlfriend's scent.

"Ash—"

There was a sickening crunch and the fae collapsed on the floor.

"Never mind," the vampire breathed, ignoring the princess entirely as he stepped over the body and into the hall. "You two are perfect for each other."

MOST PEOPLE COULD NOT have withstood a direct punch to the face from a vampire. Ellanden was no exception. It took him almost two hours to wake.

"Thank you for doing this," Evie murmured for the fifth time, passing him delicately into Seth's arms. "We're not even technically supposed to see each other until the ceremony, and if I were to drag him down to the courtyard all covered in blood—"

"It's fine, don't worry about it," the shifter said quickly, glancing down as the fae's head rolled limply to the side. "I'll clean him up and little and take him through the portal myself."

"Just don't tell Cosette," she reminded him again, unwilling to risk the woodland princess' wrath. "Or Freya, or Gran, or…or anyone else. In fact, maybe you could hide him in a cloak—"

The fae stirred weakly, trying to lift his head.

"What…what happened?"

Silver lining.

"Don't tell Ellanden either," she whispered, taking full advantage of what promised to be a delightfully convenient concussion. "Just say he slipped on the stairs."

Seth gave her a hard look. "Go."

"Thank you!" she said again, hurrying out the door. "I'll see you both there!"

She was already halfway down the hall by the time the fae opened his eyes, blinking sleepily at the shifter and wondering why his legs were dragging on the floor.

"Hey, buddy," Seth's voice echoed after her. "You think you can stand?"

CONSIDERING WHAT IT was, there was very little fanfare with the portal. Most of the rest of the city had already passed through, and almost all that remained were supplies.

Gran looked as exhausted as the princess had ever seen when she hurried across the courtyard—sliding to a stop right in front of the glowing arch.

"You're cutting it close."

Evie tossed back her hair, making a wasted effort to compose herself. "Let's be honest, it's not like they could start without me."

The old woman's eyes danced in the light. "Or my grandson. You wouldn't happen to have seen him?"

The princess' face cleared with perfect innocence.

"He didn't go through yet? That's wildly irresponsible." She took a step forward, preparing to depart. "You should really talk to him about that."

Gran tilted her head with a wry smile. "Have fun, dearie."

"See you on the other side!"

Evie stepped into the archway, but glanced over her shoulder at the same time—suddenly wondering about the prophecy, suddenly wondering if she'd ever see the Ivory City again.

She was still gazing at the shining citadel when the world around her started to fade...

Chapter 14

It had been ten years since the princess had set foot in the High Kingdom. Ten long years since she'd laid eyes on her childhood home. The very shape of it had haunted her dreams: the drawbridge, the colors, the flowers, the smells. Even trapped in the sorcerer's enchantment, a mere mention of it would fill her with such longing that she'd whisper it in her sleep for weeks to come.

Now that the moment was finally upon her, the beloved castle didn't disappoint. A breeze picked up the second she set eyes upon it as the gateway behind her sealed shut in a burst of sparks.

Home, sweet home.

Evie dropped to her knees...and threw up.

"Blasted portals," a familiar voice chimed in her ear, "they get you every time."

A helping hand appeared in front of her and she squinted up to see Kailas' smiling face, radiant and glowing in the light of the fading sun.

"What are you doing here?" she mumbled, fighting another wave of nausea. "I thought you went through ages ago."

"I promised your mother I'd wait." He waited until she look a bit steadier, then lifted her gently to her feet. "At any rate, did you honestly think you could slip through unnoticed? You wear a crown in this castle, sweetheart. There are people keeping track of where you are."

Let's hope the same isn't true for Ellanden.

"I wasn't trying to stall," she said preemptively, leaning heavily against him as she limped across the grass. "There were just some things that...some things...why do we even *have* portals?"

He chuckled as she slumped into the grass, clutching her head as the world spun.

"People say it's better than flying for three days," he answered easily. She shot him an incredulous look, and he held up both hands. "You'll never hear me saying that. Although, in their defense, it might be more enjoyable if you get to *be* the dragon..."

She tried to laugh, but ended up groaning. "Seriously, I feel like death."

"Take all the time you need," he said lightly, sitting down beside her in the grass. "I'm in no hurry..."

She shot him a secret look, wondering why he'd lingered in the forest for over two hours waiting for her. Wondering if perhaps she wasn't the only one who'd been stalling after all.

"Is it ever hard for you," she asked suddenly, "coming back to this castle?"

She wouldn't have blamed him.

Not only had he spent his entire adolescence trapped in a dark enchantment, being forced to play monster all over the realm, but he was also the only Damaris to have slept in the dungeons.

He glanced at her in surprise. "Why do you ask?"

She shrugged, feeling a bit steadier. "When I was growing up, you spent more time in Taviel and Vale then you did in your own palace. I never really wondered why that was until now."

He considered this a moment before turning back to the castle. "Sometimes it's hard. There are certain places I don't go. Certain stairwells...corridors that lead to the lower levels."

She stared at him cautiously, not wanting to push too far. "So you have specific memories of it? Alwyn's enchantment?"

The prince flinched ever so slightly, as he always did upon hearing the wizard's name. Talk of such time had always been scarce, and was generally discouraged by the other adults.

"Most memories happened away from the castle," he admitted. "But I have a few. They get easier to remember once I started sneaking to the dungeons to see Sera. I remember the day he caught me coming back up the stairs, asked me what I was doing..."

He trailed off with that faraway look he sometimes got. Only this time his beautiful wife wasn't there to take his hand, to coax him back to the light.

"Why do you ask?" he said a bit sharply.

Her cheeks flushed and she dropped her eyes.

"I can't remember anything from the wizard's cave," she admitted. "I remember falling asleep and waking up again...but nothing in between. I keep trying...but everything goes blank."

Most of what survived from the enchantment had been feelings—a perpetual chill, an overall sense of something being not well. Sometimes she thought she remembered a clawed hand reaching out to her in the dark—curling its fingers around her face.

Kailas softened immediately, looking down with concern. "Do you want to remember?"

She thought about it a moment, then bowed her head.

"I don't know...sometimes." She paused, then continued suddenly. "Sometimes, it just makes me angry. That so much time was wasted, that so many things were beyond my control."

She drifted back, suppressing a shiver.

"Sometimes I feel like it might be easier if I'd learned something. If there had been some big lesson that could justify all that lost time..."

Her uncle was quiet for a while, then he pushed to his feet.

"I can understand that," he said gently, offering a hand. "I didn't get any lessons either. But I did get a kind of...certainty, I suppose. That's something I would never trade."

She stood off the grass. "...Aunt Sera?"

He flashed a melancholy smile. "She was my light. Bringing me out of that darkness, time after time."

A WEDDING IN THE HIGH Kingdom was always a festive affair. If that wedding happened to involve a member of the royal family, it would be a spectacle one could never forget.

But if that wedding came on the eve of battle...it was decidedly more subdued.

There would be no crowds and no parades. No tournaments or balls. No foreign dignitaries offering tribute, and no heated arguments over seating arrangements and types of Champagne.

It would be a small ceremony. Just a few hundred people.

Simple dress, simple rings, simple flowers.

Perfect.

Evie stood in front of the mirror, watching as a servant she didn't recognize put the final touches on her hair. She didn't recognize most of the servants. At first she'd though there must have been some kind of sickness, or another such explanation to have wiped them all out.

Not until later did she realize the servants *were* the same ones she'd grown up with...only they were ten years older, while she'd stayed exactly the same.

"I believe that's all, milady. Unless you require anything else?"

Evie shook her head quickly, dismissing the woman with a tight smile.

Upon her insistence, the preparations had been kept to a minimum. If asked, she could have easily used their imminent voyage to the Dunes as an excuse, but in truth she couldn't stomach getting dolled up for such an event. She'd rather come as she was—a kingdom, not a bride.

Her face had been painted to perfection and a delicate tiara had been pinned into her waving hair. The dress itself was a simple white sheath—elegant and rather refreshingly plain.

Adelaide had sat with her as she was getting ready, forcing pained smiles and dabbing at her eyes. Cosette had sat with her, too, until she was whisked away to the ceremony.

At the end of the day, there weren't many people left in the castle. Just the bride and the groom.

Unless he's already gone outside...

Like something out of a dream, the princess drifted down the hall and towards the fae's usual chambers, half-surprised when the sound of quiet voices drifted through the door.

"—this is getting pathetic."

She peeked her head inside to see Ellanden and his father standing on the balcony. One was looking rather amused, the other was waging a one-handed war against his hair.

"I've almost got it."

The young fae had apparently managed to dislodge the diamond necklace by tearing loose the thin braids strung through his ivory locks. It was only when he attempted weaving them back together again that he suddenly remembered a vampire had massacred his hand.

"You're making everything much worse," Cassiel said with an amused smile, watching as his son tilted precariously for a better angle. "And we're short on time. Just let me help you."

"It's fine," Ellanden snapped. "I can do it myself."

Any other day, the princess would have laughed at the sight. While the fae always had braids in his hair, she'd never imagined him actually braiding it—as if they just appeared each morning.

But try as he might, the task was clearly beyond him.

"Seriously, I've almost got it—"

Cassiel circled around behind him, easing the hair from his son's angry hands and deftly weaving it together with his own skilled fingers. In a matter of seconds, it began to take shape.

"I haven't done this since you were a child," Cassiel murmured with a smile. "I could never get you to sit still long enough for me to finish."

The prince grinned in spite of himself, staring into the golden sky.

"I remember."

The rest of the castle may have been eagerly awaiting the ceremony, milling about the lawns in fragrance of a thousand enchanting flowers from the immortal city, but on the balcony in the western tower, time seemed to have paused. Evie watched in a kind of trance as the fae stood side by side, watching as that golden sunset dripped slowly across the sky.

"You have no idea how many times I'd do this when you were away," Cassiel murmured quietly. "Watching day fade into night...wondering where you were, what you were doing, what might be happening to you." There was a hitch in his breathing. "You have no idea how many times I wished I could close my eyes and just...appear wherever you might be."

Ellanden bowed his head, leaning against him. "You have no idea how any times I wished that myself."

Since returning to Taviel, a hint of his old accent had crept back into his voice. A lilting way of phrasing that wasn't rooted in place so much as it was in time. The princess had always teased him when they were younger, but the truth was she'd always been jealous of how it sounded.

Like he'd come from a fairytale, stepped right off the page.

"It was different than how I expected," Ellanden continued suddenly, "going off on an adventure of my own." He smiled faintly, as if at his own silliness. But it stilled upon his face when he looked back over the lawns. "I never thought it would end like this."

Cassiel's eyes tightened with a look of physical pain.

"It doesn't *need* to end like this," he said quietly. "You don't need to marry her, Landi. Not if you love another. There are other ways—"

"But this is the best way," Ellanden interrupted softly. "We both know that to be true."

The princess slipped unnoticed from the doorway, easing back into the hall.

Words that every bride wishes to hear...

A rather odd turn of events, but truth be told she couldn't be offended. They hadn't said anything that she hadn't been feeling herself. If anything, it was oddly comforting that everyone was on the same page, that there would be no posturing or false expectations.

It truly was an alliance...nothing more.

I haven't even seen the ring, she realized as she drifted back down the hall. *I suppose someone will hand that to me when the time comes—*

"Mace!"

She stepped back in surprise, staring at the faithful shifter.

Since the days she was born her famed Belarian protector had been shadowing her every step, following her from kingdom to kingdom. She shouldn't have been surprised to see him now.

"Milady." He spoke softly and bowed low, just as he'd always done.

"I didn't realize...I didn't realize you had stayed in the High Kingdom."

He nodded his head.

"It was the last place I had seen you alive, milady," he answered softly. "And after so much time...it had started to feel like home."

She tried to smile, but it froze on her face. "And Hastings?"

They had always come in a pair, her two guards. A knight from the High Kingdom and a wolf from Belaria. Never was one seen without the other.

He bowed his head again, lips pressed into a thin line.

"Gone."

No other explanation was given. The princess didn't have the heart to require it. Ten years ago, she might have broken down—but that girl had grown up quite a bit since her time on the road. She took a moment to process, eyes filling with tears before setting it aside to grieve on a later day.

"Have you come to escort me?" she asked instead, listening to the distant bells.

"Yes, milady." He gestured to the massive oak doors that led to the lawn. "To a knight, who will escort you to your father. His Majesty the king will escort you the rest of the way."

She set off once again before suddenly whirling back around..

"I heard you calling," she confessed. "That day by the river...I heard you calling me back."

Like it was yesterday, she heard those lupine howls echoing through the trees. Each one had torn straight into her. Each one had seared itself so deeply, she could never forget.

The shifter nodded slowly, staring into her eyes. "I have been tasked with protecting you, milady. But it seems that you have been tasked with protecting us all. I hope you will not think me rude to say it...but that makes me very proud."

She squeezed his hand, then the two continued outside.

THE SUN HAD NEARLY set by the time the princess left the castle, and right on cue she heard the bells chiming to announce the start. A tall man was waiting for her in the grass, the knight to escort her, another person she didn't recognize, until he turned around and she let out a gasp.

"...Thomas?!"

What seemed like a few weeks ago Thomas McCallen had been sitting beside her in class, trying his best to flirt, blushing painfully every time she glanced his way. They'd been born the same year. Every feast day since they were children, he'd work up the courage to ask her to dance.

He flashed a boyish grin.

"When I heard you needed a knight from your own kingdom, I volunteered."

She shook her head in amazement. "You are a knight."

Like you always wanted to be.

He smiled again, gesturing to the armor. He filled it out nicely. A far cry from the boy with the sickly complexion and stick-thin legs. "Not all of us could stay young forever. Shall we?"

She took his arm and they continued walking towards the crowd of people gathered on the other side of the lawn. From such a distance, she could just barely make out the rest of her family, waiting for her beneath a flowering arch. Ellanden was there as well, standing in the center.

Thomas followed her gaze with a thoughtful expression. "I guess we all knew it would be Ellanden. Although, to be honest, I had always thought..."

Her eyes drifted over the crowd, but there wasn't a vampire in sight. Every single person she'd ever loved was gathered in the same place, at the same time...with one enormous exception.

This isn't right. It's not supposed to end this way.

They stopped halfway between the castle and the altar. From there, her father was supposed to walk her the rest of the way. He was already coming towards them, moving with a stiff smile.

"It's quiet," Evie muttered, almost to herself. "I don't know that I've ever heard it so quiet."

Thomas glanced at the top of her head.

"I suppose they've commanded that for you," he joked, watching the king approach. "At any rate, we should probably go a bit further. We don't want to make him—"

He let out a sudden cough, an odd expression on his face.

"Thomas?"

They stared at each other, then looked down at the crimson stains all over her white dress.

What the...?

She was still lifting a finger, when she saw the arrow. Pitch black and thick as a spade, lodged right in the center of his chest. He fell in what felt like slow motion, dead before he hit the grass.

A scream rose in her throat, but the rest of them never heard it. Because at that precise moment, the forest opened and everyone else started screaming just the same.

We were waiting to start the war ourselves? We were fools.

A volley of dark arrows shot out of the sky.

It has already begun...

THE END

Enchanted – Book 11 – Blurb

OLD ENEMIES PROWL, for the dead never die…

When Evie Damaris' wedding is interrupted, the four kingdoms must rally together. But the army Kaleb Grey has gathered against them isn't as it seems. New friends are pitted against old foes, and with most of their own forces still leagues away from the High Kingdom, it seems as though the battle may be already lost.

An unlikely proposition throws the fate of the realm out of balance, while a new set of players enters the field. The search for the stone reaches a turning point, but those wedding bells still chime in the distance.

Can Evie and her friends mend their broken fellowship? Can a turn of good faith mend the same hurts in the realm? Or will the dark tide they've been holding back finally overwhelm them all…?

The Queen's Alpha Series

Eternal
Everlasting
Unceasing
Evermore
Forever
Boundless
Prophecy
Protected
Foretelling
Revelation
Betrayal
Resolved

The Omega Queen Series

Discipline
Bravery
Courage
Conquer
Strength
Validation
Approval
Blessing
Balance
Grievance
Enchanted
Gratified

The Beginning's End Series

– COMING SOON –
Excerpt included

BEGINNING'S END SERIES
BEGINNINGS

USA Today Bestselling Author
W.J. MAY

EXCERPT

Beginnings Blurb

Book 1 of the Beginning's End Series

You've read the ending, but there is a beginning to every story…
Centuries before the creation of the five kingdoms, when the great houses were still forming and the realm was ruled by the fae, a small band of companions set out on a journey.

Kiera had never left her village. It was a stroke of luck that she wasn't there when the dragon attacked. Without any friends or family, without a shred of hope that anyone might believe her, she strikes off alone into the forest, looking for people that can help.

The world is new and untamed. The people are leaderless and wild. There has never been an alliance to unite them, but an alliance is exactly what the realm needs.

Because a darkness is coming. One that threatens to consume them all…

Chapter 1 Beginnings

"Those fish heads aren't going to chop themselves!"

The girl stared down at her hands. Pale from too little sunlight. Scarred from cooking over an open fire. Beneath the grease stains were callouses reserved for those who gripped reins all day, or devoted their lives to the swing of a sword. She'd gotten hers from decapitating fish.

"Kiera!"

She startled back to the present as a door swung open and the sounds of a crowded tavern filtered inside. A discordant chorus of voices, punctuated every few seconds with a deafening shout for *more ale*. Those two words haunted her dreams. It didn't help that she slept above the tavern.

"Nice of you to join us."

The man scowling in the doorway could hardly be counted as a man at all. While the general shape was there, he was sporting an extra three feet in every direction. It made him invaluable as the proprietor of such a rowdy establishment, and somewhat difficult when it came to stairs.

"The fish," he repeated slowly, as if she couldn't be counted on to remember. "I needed that stew to be ready ages ago. The people are hungry."

That stew will make them ill.

Instead of voicing this opinion aloud, she gave a sarcastic salute and poured a bucket of freshly caught trout upon the counter, grabbing a cleaver as the man slipped back through the door.

I shouldn't have done that.

Her cheeks flushed with belated guilt, as she gave the blade a cursory rinse.

She was lucky to have a job. So many people didn't. Since scraping its way through an especially bleak winter, work in the tiny village had been scarce. Fortunately, for all his menace and bluster, the proprietor was actually a good man. He kept her on staff. And no matter what might be happening in the rest of the world, there remained a universal truth: people always needed a drink.

With the skilled hands of one who'd done it many times before, she positioned the fish and swung the blade fiercely, imagining each one to be the face of a recent patron. A goblin who tried to walk out on his bill. A shifter who'd grabbed her around the waist as she tried to pass by.

There were more than enough to keep her occupied, and before long, she was hacking merrily away—dreaming now of bigger things: ogres and giants and trolls. Some people might fend them off with swords and spears, but she didn't need anything more than her handy cleaver. They fell, one after the other, crumbling to the ground in a revolting display of blood and gore. Some tried to flee in terror, before feeling the kiss of her deadly blade. Some were screaming for—

"More ale!"

She paused with the cleaver still raised above her, a ribbon of amphibious blood trailing up the inside of her arm. The fish were quickly abandoned, dumped into a large pot, as she hurried out of the kitchen and back to the main bar—grabbing two pitchers as she went.

Marcel, her fellow bartender, was in the corner with some fishermen, trying to settle was quickly escalating into a violent dispute. Talbot, the proprietor, had taken his place behind the bar, watching the crowd with one eye, as the other measured the drinks.

"Busy night," he murmured, unfazed by the general clamor as he continued to pour. "Did you finish with the fish?"

She swept up beside him, tying back her hair.

"I annihilated them..."

He chuckled under his breath, flicking a piece of tail from her shoulder, then quickly easing the frothing pitchers from her hand. "It's too festive out there tonight. Why don't you stay behind the counter? Pour the whiskey. Let me handle the ale."

Festive. Tavern code for: dangerous. It was the word they used when it was a little too full, tempers were a little too heated, and the men had already been served a little too much whiskey.

Marcel had no such codes, but he didn't need them. The man was part shifter.

"Are you sure?" she asked, trying to hide her relief. "It's no problem."

The man nodded, squinting slightly, like he'd gotten something in his eye. It was a dance they'd done many times. A brusque series of grunts and deflections, hiding the affection beneath.

He was gone a moment later, leaving her alone behind the bar.

END OF EXCERPT
BEGINNINGS
COMING SOON

Find W.J. May

Website:
http://www.wjmaybooks.com
Facebook:
https://www.facebook.com/pages/Author-WJ-May-FAN-PAGE/141170442608149
Newsletter:
SIGN UP FOR W.J. May's Newsletter to find out about new releases, updates, cover reveals and even freebies!
http://eepurl.com/97aYf

More books by W.J. May

The Chronicles of Kerrigan
BOOK I - *Rae of Hope* is FREE!
Book Trailer:
http://www.youtube.com/watch?v=gILAwXxx8MU
Book II - *Dark Nebula*
Book Trailer:
http://www.youtube.com/watch?v=Ca24STi_bFM
Book III - *House of Cards*
Book IV - *Royal Tea*
Book V - *Under Fire*
Book VI - *End in Sight*
Book VII – *Hidden Darkness*
Book VIII – *Twisted Together*
Book IX – *Mark of Fate*
Book X – *Strength & Power*
Book XI – *Last One Standing*
BOOK XII – *Rae of Light*

PREQUEL –
Christmas Before the Magic
Question the Darkness
Into the Darkness
Fight the Darkness
Alone the Darkness
Lost the Darkness

SEQUEL –
    Matter of Time
    Time Piece
    Second Chance
    Glitch in Time
    Our Time
    Precious Time

Hidden Secrets Saga:
Download Seventh Mark part 1 For FREE
Book Trailer:
http://www.youtube.com/watch?v=Y-_vVYC1gvo

Like most teenagers, Rouge is trying to figure out who she is and what she wants to be. With little knowledge about her past, she has questions but has never tried to find the answers. Everything changes when she befriends a strangely intoxicating family. Siblings Grace and Michael, appear to have secrets which seem connected to Rouge. Her hunch is confirmed when a horrible incident occurs at an outdoor party. Rouge may be the only one who can find the answer.

An ancient journal, a Sioghra necklace and a special mark force life-altering decisions for a girl who grew up unprepared to fight for her life or others.

All secrets have a cost and Rouge's determination to find the truth can only lead to trouble...or something even more sinister.

RADIUM HALOS - THE SENSELESS SERIES
Book 1 is FREE

Everyone needs to be a hero at one point in their life.

The small town of Elliot Lake will never be the same again.

Caught in a sudden thunderstorm, Zoe, a high school senior from Elliot Lake, and five of her friends take shelter in an abandoned uranium mine. Over the next few days, Zoe's hearing sharpens drastically, beyond what any normal human being can detect. She tells her friends, only to learn that four others have an increased sense as well. Only Kieran, the new boy from Scotland, isn't affected.

Fashioning themselves into superheroes, the group tries to stop the strange occurrences happening in their little town. Muggings, break-ins, disappearances, and murder begin to hit too close to home. It leads the team to think someone knows about their secret - someone who wants them all dead.

An incredulous group of heroes. A traitor in the midst. Some dreams are written in blood.

Courage Runs Red
The Blood Red Series
Book 1 is FREE

WHAT IF COURAGE WAS your only option?

When Kallie lands a college interview with the city's new hot-shot police officer, she has no idea everything in her life is about to change. The detective is young, handsome and seems to have an unnatural ability to stop the increasing local crime rate. Detective Liam's particular interest in Kallie sends her heart and head stumbling over each other.

When a raging blood feud between vampires spills into her home, Kallie gets caught in the middle. Torn between love and family loyalty she must find the courage to fight what she fears the most and possibly risk everything, even if it means dying for those she loves.

Daughter of Darkness - Victoria
Only Death Could Stop Her Now
The Daughters of Darkness is a series of female heroines who may or may not know each other, but all have the same father, Vlad Montour. Victoria is a Hunter Vampire

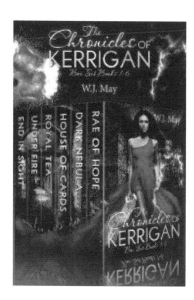

Don't miss out!

Visit the website below and you can sign up to receive emails whenever W.J. May publishes a new book. There's no charge and no obligation.

https://books2read.com/r/B-A-SSF-HTROB

BOOKS 2 READ

Connecting independent readers to independent writers.

Did you love *Grievance*? Then you should read *Omega Queen - Box Set Books #1-3*[1] by W.J. May!

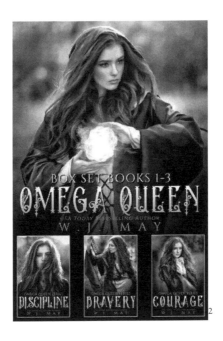

[2]

USA Today Bestselling author, W.J. May, brings you the Omega Box Set for a limited time. This YA/NA series covers love, betrayal, coming of age, magic and fantasy.

Be prepared to fight, it's the only option.

BOOK 1 - DISCIPLINE

Not every fairytale has a happily ever after...

For the first time in hundreds of years, the five kingdoms were at peace. United by the band of young heroes who'd won the Great War, the realm had entered a time of wealth and prosperity unlike anything it had known before. New families. New Beginnings. Old alliances were on the mend.

---

1. https://books2read.com/u/b6OJ2E

2. https://books2read.com/u/b6OJ2E

But such a thing can never last.

When Katerina and Dylan's teenage daughter finds herself at the center of a strange prediction, she and her friends are swept away on a wild adventure that may very well claim all of their lives. Old evils are lurking the shadows. A secret new darkness is waiting to take hold.

Can the new band of heroes stop it in time?

Or has their happily ever after finally come to an end?

BOOK 2 - BRAVERY

How long can you outrun your fate?

When Evie and her friends set out to fulfill a long-awaited prophecy, they never thought their adventure would turn into a nightmare before their very eyes.

Trapped in a cavern beneath the ground, they find themselves going up against a creature so twisted and terrible, they wouldn't have believed it was real. Their strength is tested and friendships are strained. But as they soon discover, the creature was the least of their problems.

The world is shifting. Shadows and darkness are entering the land. Rumors are whispering around the remaining kingdoms. Rumors of a dark and powerful stone.

Can the friends find it in time? Or are some prophecies never meant to be?

BOOK 3 - COURAGE

How time flies...

When Evie and her friends find themselves trapped in the sorcerer's cave, they think all is lost. But rescue comes from the most unlikely of people. And with it comes the most terrible truth.

With the five kingdoms divided and the realm on the verge of collapse, the prophecy is more urgent than ever. But the road is treacherous and the friends are on the other side of the realm. New alliances must be forged and friendships are tested as they set off to fulfill their destiny, only to find that the fates may have something different in store.

Is it possible to pick up the pieces and start again? Can the friends get to the Dunes and find the missing stone in time?

More importantly...

...are some sins too terrible to forgive?

Be careful who you trust.

Even the devil was once an angel.

OMEGA QUEEN SERIES

Discipline

Bravery

Courage

Conquer

Strength

Validation

Approval

Blessing

Balance

Grievance

Enchanted

Gratified

ORIGINAL SERIES:

Queen's Alpha Series: Eternal

Everlasting

Unceasing

Evermore

Forever

Boundless

Prophecy

Protected

Foretelling

Revelation

Betrayal

Resolved

Read more at www.wjmaybooks.com.

Also by W.J. May

Bit-Lit Series
Lost Vampire
Cost of Blood
Price of Death

Blood Red Series
Courage Runs Red
The Night Watch
Marked by Courage
Forever Night
The Other Side of Fear
Blood Red Box Set Books #1-5

Daughters of Darkness: Victoria's Journey
Victoria
Huntress
Coveted (A Vampire & Paranormal Romance)
Twisted
Daughter of Darkness - Victoria - Box Set

Great Temptation Series
The Devil's Footsteps
Heaven's Command
Mortals Surrender

Hidden Secrets Saga
Seventh Mark - Part 1
Seventh Mark - Part 2
Marked By Destiny
Compelled
Fate's Intervention
Chosen Three
The Hidden Secrets Saga: The Complete Series

Kerrigan Chronicles
Stopping Time
A Passage of Time
Ticking Clock
Secrets in Time
Time in the City
Ultimate Future

Kerrigan Memoirs
Chronicles of Devon

Mending Magic Series
Lost Souls
Illusion of Power
Challenging the Dark
Castle of Power
Limits of Magic
Protectors of Light

Omega Queen Series
Discipline
Bravery
Courage
Conquer
Strength
Validation
Approval
Blessing
Balance
Grievance
Omega Queen - Box Set Books #1-3

Paranormal Huntress Series
Never Look Back
Coven Master
Alpha's Permission
Blood Bonding
Oracle of Nightmares
Shadows in the Night

Paranormal Huntress BOX SET

Prophecy Series
Only the Beginning
White Winter
Secrets of Destiny

Revamped Series
Hidden
Banished
Converted

Royal Factions
The Price For Peace
The Cost for Surviving
The Punishment For Deception
Faking Perfection
The Most Cherished
The Strength to Endure

The Chronicles of Kerrigan
Rae of Hope
Dark Nebula
House of Cards
Royal Tea
Under Fire

End in Sight
Hidden Darkness
Twisted Together
Mark of Fate
Strength & Power
Last One Standing
Rae of Light
The Chronicles of Kerrigan Box Set Books # 1 - 6

The Chronicles of Kerrigan: Gabriel
Living in the Past
Present For Today
Staring at the Future

The Chronicles of Kerrigan Prequel
Christmas Before the Magic
Question the Darkness
Into the Darkness
Fight the Darkness
Alone in the Darkness
Lost in Darkness
The Chronicles of Kerrigan Prequel Series Books #1-3

The Chronicles of Kerrigan Sequel
A Matter of Time
Time Piece
Second Chance
Glitch in Time

Our Time
Precious Time

The Hidden Secrets Saga
Seventh Mark (part 1 & 2)

The Kerrigan Kids
School of Potential
Myths & Magic
Kith & Kin
Playing With Power
Line of Ancestry
Descent of Hope
Illusion of Shadows
Frozen by the Future
Guilt Of My Past
Demise of Magic
Rise of The Prophecy
The Kerrigan Kids Box Set Books #1-3

The Queen's Alpha Series
Eternal
Everlasting
Unceasing
Evermore
Forever
Boundless
Prophecy

Protected
Foretelling
Revelation
Betrayal
Resolved
The Queen's Alpha Box Set

The Senseless Series
Radium Halos - Part 1
Radium Halos - Part 2
Nonsense
Perception
The Senseless - Box Set Books #1-4

Standalone
Shadow of Doubt (Part 1 & 2)
Five Shades of Fantasy
Zwarte Nevel
Shadow of Doubt - Part 1
Shadow of Doubt - Part 2
Four and a Half Shades of Fantasy
Dream Fighter
What Creeps in the Night
Forest of the Forbidden
Arcane Forest: A Fantasy Anthology
The First Fantasy Box Set

Watch for more at www.wjmaybooks.com.

About the Author

About W.J. May

Welcome to USA TODAY BESTSELLING author W.J. May's Page! SIGN UP for W.J. May's Newsletter to find out about new releases, updates, cover reveals and even freebies! http://eepurl.com/97aYf

Website: http://www.wjmaybooks.com

Facebook: http://www.facebook.com/pages/Author-WJ-May-FAN-PAGE/141170442608149?ref=hl *Please feel free to connect with me and share your comments. I love connecting with my readers.*

W.J. May grew up in the fruit belt of Ontario. Crazy-happy childhood, she always has had a vivid imagination and loads of energy. After her father passed away in 2008, from a six-year battle with cancer (which she still believes he won the fight against), she began to write again. A passion she'd loved for years, but realized life was too short to keep putting it off. She is a writer of Young Adult, Fantasy Fiction and where ever else her little muses take her.

Read more at www.wjmaybooks.com.

Made in the USA
Columbia, SC
02 January 2022